# Mariela in the Desert

by Karen Zacarías

---

**FOR PRODUCTION INQUIRIES**

UNITED STATES AND CANADA
info@concordtheatricals.com
1-866-979-0447

UNITED KINGDOM AND EUROPE
licensing@concordtheatricals.co.uk
020-7054-7298

Each title is subject to availability from Concord Theatricals Corp., depending upon country of performance. Please be aware that *MARIELA IN THE DESERT* may not be licensed by Concord Theatricals Corp. in your territory. Professional and amateur producers should contact the nearest Concord Theatricals Corp. office or licensing partner to verify availability.

---

No one shall make any changes in this title(s) for the purpose of production. No part of this book may be reproduced, stored in a retrieval system, scanned, uploaded, or transmitted in any form, by any means, now known or yet to be invented, including mechanical, electronic, digital, photocopying, recording, videotaping, or otherwise, without the prior written permission of the publisher. No one shall share this title(s), or any part of this title(s), through any social media or file hosting websites.

For all inquiries regarding motion picture, television, online/digital and other media rights, please contact Concord Theatricals Corp.

## MUSIC AND THIRD-PARTY MATERIALS USE NOTE

Licensees are solely responsible for obtaining formal written permission from copyright owners to use copyrighted music and/or other copyrighted third-party materials (e.g. artworks, logos) in the performance of this play and are strongly cautioned to do so. If no such permission is obtained by the licensee, then the licensee must use only original music and materials that the licensee owns and controls. Licensees are solely responsible and liable for clearances of all third-party copyrighted materials, including without limitation music, and shall indemnify the copyright owners of the play(s) and their licensing agent, Concord Theatricals Corp., against any costs, expenses, losses and liabilities arising from the use of such copyrighted third-party materials by licensees. For music, please contact the appropriate music licensing authority in your territory for the rights to any incidental music.

## IMPORTANT BILLING AND CREDIT REQUIREMENTS

If you have obtained performance rights to this title, please refer to your licensing agreement for important billing and credit requirements.

*MARIELA IN THE DESERT* had its world premiere at The Goodman Theatre in Chicago, Illinois in January 2005. The performance was directed by Henry Godinez. The scenic and projection design was by John Boesche. Costume design was by Jacqueline Firkins and lighting design was by Robert Christen. Sound design was by Andre Pluess and Ben Sussman. Original music was by Gustavo Leone, and the dramaturgs were Lenora Inez Brown and Tom Creamer. The Production Stage Manager was Kimberly Osgood. The cast was as follows:

**MARIELA** ........................................Sandra Marquez
**JOSÉ** ........................................... Ricardo Gutiérrez
**OLIVA** ............................................... Laura Crotte
**BLANCA** ........................................ Sandra Delgado
**CARLOS** ...................................... Eric Lloyd Ambriz
**ADAM** ............................................... Mark Ulrich

*MARIELA IN THE DESERT* was also produced by The Denver Center in April of 2010. The performance was directed by Bruce Sevy. Original music was composed by Gregg Coffin. The scenic design was by Vicki Smith and the costume design was by Clint Ramos. The lighting design was by Don Darnutzer and the sound design was by William Burns. Projection design was by Charlie I. Miller and dramaturgy was by Douglas Langworthy. The Production Manager was Edward Lapine. The Stage Manager was A. Phoebe Sacks and the Assistant Stage Manager was D. Lynn Reiland. The Production Intern was Steven Dalton. The cast was as follows:

**MARIELA** ........................................Yetta Gottesman
**JOSÉ** ..............................................Robert Sicular
**OLIVA** ....................................Franca Sofia Barchiesi
**BLANCA** ............................................. Vivia Font
**CARLOS** ..................................... Jean-Pierre Serret
**ADAM** ..............................................Sam Gregory

*MARIELA IN THE DESERT* was originally commissioned by South Coast Repertory Company.

# CHARACTERS

**MARIELA** – A wry, beautiful, strong woman who used to paint. Age: forty to forty-five.

**JOSÉ** – Her husband. A famous artist. Age: fifty to sixties.

**OLIVA** – José's pious older sister. Age: fifty to sixty-five.

**BLANCA** – Mariela's and José's talented and vulnerable daughter. Age: twenty-one. (Also plays Blanca as a child.)

**CARLOS** – The son who has disappeared. Blanca's younger brother. Eighteen. Also plays Carlos as a child.

**ADAM** – Jewish-American Art History professor teaching in Mexico City. Blanca's lover. Age: thirty-five to forty-five.

# SETTING

Mexico.

# TIME

1951.

# AUTHOR'S NOTES

A rustic ranch in the Northern Mexican desert region: no running water, kerosene lamps and candles.

Time and place should be fluid. The desert is present...it bleeds into the house.

# ACT I

*(One single painting – with a large violent slit down the middle – faces upstage.)*

*(Focus on **JOSÉ**, Mariela's husband, in a bed. **MARIELA** enters, removes her black shawl, hands it to **OLIVA**, her sister-in-law. **OLIVA** hands her a pan of water. **OLIVA** exits. **MARIELA** faces the bed where her husband **JOSÉ** is lying. **MARIELA** prepares to bathe and dress her husband. She traces his face with the wash cloth.)*

**JOSÉ**.  Damn, that's cold.

**MARIELA**.  The doctor said that cold water –

**JOSÉ**.  Damn the doctors. They themselves should have to do everything they prescribe for the patient. Keeps them honest.

**MARIELA**.  Our daughter is coming home.

**JOSÉ**.  *(Beat.)* So you wrote the telegram?

**MARIELA**.  I paid an exorbitant fee. The man said that it would reach Blanca in Mexico City today.

**JOSÉ**.  You were gone all day.

**MARIELA**.  The closest telegraph is far away. And the roads are cracked and ragged. On the way back, the driver had to stop and help push a poor cow out of the way.

**JOSÉ**.  You left me all alone.

**MARIELA**.  Oliva is here.

**JOSÉ**. My sister doesn't count. You were gone so long the sun must be setting. What color is the sky?

**MARIELA**. A thin line of crimson – a smear of dirty rose. A winter sky.

**JOSÉ**. The desert is God's canvas.

**MARIELA**. That always sounds prettier than it feels.

**JOSÉ**. Anything new in town?

**MARIELA**. The telegraph office has a brand new black and white sign, with the new higher prices in bright red. But a large glob of paint ran amok so most of the numbers are smeared and illegible.

**JOSÉ**. You could say it's a sign of progress.

**MARIELA**. Or you can say: it's just a sign.

**JOSÉ**. *(Beat.)* You think Blanca will come this time?

**MARIELA**. Yes. I do.

**JOSÉ**. *(Pause.)* What did you write?

**MARIELA**. I was persuasive.

**JOSÉ**. Did you tell her I was very sick?

**MARIELA**. Somewhat. Can I bathe you?

**JOSÉ**. Did you tell her that I am slowly going blind? That I have trouble walking? That I have to lie in this God-forsaken bed most of the day? – No bath! I am not getting clean for nothing.

**MARIELA**. I told her you were dead.

**JOSÉ**. What?

**MARIELA**. I told Blanca you were dead.

**JOSÉ**. Mariela!

**MARIELA**. Yes. Dead.

**JOSÉ**. A little premature, don't you think?

**MARIELA.** I wrote that I would wait to bury you until she came.

**JOSÉ.** Why in the world would you write something like that?

**MARIELA.** She's ignored all our entreaties to come home. But the death of her father might get her attention.

**JOSÉ.** You shouldn't frighten her like that.

**MARIELA.** On the contrary, my love. Think of how of happy she'll be to see you alive.

**JOSÉ.** What did you write?

**MARIELA.** *(Pulls out a copy of the telegram.)* Blanca, my dearest daughter. STOP

All is well here. STOP

Except your father is dead. STOP

Come home. STOP

I won't bury him without you. STOP

Hurry. It's hot. END

**JOSÉ.** My God!

**MARIELA.** Blanca needs to see you. She will hate herself if she doesn't see you before you die.

**JOSÉ.** Why not just tell her that I'm very sick?

**MARIELA.** José, you've been sick for so long, it doesn't feel like news. Now let me bathe you.

**JOSÉ.** Fine. Don't overdo the soap. It makes me itch.

**MARIELA.** Then scratch, old man.

**JOSÉ.** If you hadn't driven her away –

**MARIELA.** I didn't drive her away; I sent her to school in Mexico City.

**JOSÉ**. She was fifteen years old! Alone and unprotected in the big city.

**MARIELA**. My cousins took very good care of her.

**JOSÉ**. She was grieving. Carlos had just died.

**MARIELA**. It was the right thing to do. She needed to be with people her own age.

**JOSÉ**. She was learning more here with us.

**MARIELA**. Stuck here in the middle of paradise? Miles away from other children? She came home every summer, every Christmas.

**JOSÉ**. Something happened. It's been two years since we've seen her.

**MARIELA**. She started attending the university. That's what happened.

**JOSÉ**. I haven't seen my baby girl in two years.

**MARIELA**. Your baby girl is twenty-one years old.

**JOSÉ**. *(Stops her.)* You should have never sent her away.

**MARIELA**. She's coming home tonight. Let me finish bathing you.

**JOSÉ**. Why would the doctor prescribe cold water? It's archaic and barbaric.

**MARIELA**. Maybe it's exactly what you need.

**JOSÉ**. Mariela, I'm not dead.

**MARIELA**. But all good things come to those who wait.

**JOSÉ**. I have dined with important men! My paintings hang in the Governor's house. Diego Rivera borrowed money from me. Orozco drank –

**JOSÉ & MARIELA**. *(Unison.)* Liquor from my flask.

**JOSÉ**. Dammit, it's true. And I could make love to you three times a night!

*(She pulls out the insulin and the syringe.)*

**MARIELA.** It's time for your insulin shot. *(Looks at the bottle.)*

**JOSÉ.** You aren't listening to me.

**MARIELA.** Yes, I am. Three times a night. Now, turn over.

**JOSÉ.** Take your hands off me.

**MARIELA.** You heard the doctor, if you don't take your insulin, your blood will get thick and slow, your heart will stop pumping. And then, José, you really will be dead.

*(Pause.)*

**JOSÉ.** Why do you hate me?

**MARIELA.** I don't hate you.

**JOSÉ.** Our lives are not all my fault.

**MARIELA.** I never said that.

**JOSÉ.** You don't have to say anything. *(Beat.)* I'm thirsty.

*(**MARIELA** pours **JOSÉ** a glass of water from a pitcher.)*

**MARIELA.** You're always thirsty.

**JOSÉ.** The gardenia is getting brittle. It needs watering. Water the flower. It's beautiful.

**MARIELA.** But I also need to finish washing you and clean out the latrine.

**JOSÉ.** Dirt, shit or flowers. Choose wisely.

**MARIELA.** I have things I have to do.

**JOSÉ.** Stay! Talk to me. *(Pause.)* Bathe me.

**MARIELA.** All right. Now be quiet for a while.

*(Silence. She bathes him, tenderly.)*

**JOSÉ.** Will you miss me after I'm gone?

**MARIELA**.  No. *(Beat.)* Yes.

>   *(The bath is over.)*

**JOSÉ**.  So how do I look?

**MARIELA**.  *(Pause. Really looks.)* Pale and flushed...

**JOSÉ**.  That bad?

**MARIELA**.  There are thick grooves of gray in your cheeks. And your eyes are so dark and bright. To capture you on canvas right now...

**JOSÉ**.  You wouldn't dare.

**MARIELA**.  No, I wouldn't. *(Beat.)* Now, what do you want for dinner?

**JOSÉ**.  I should have been castrated the day I laid eyes on you.

**MARIELA**.  Does that mean you're not hungry?

**JOSÉ**.  Carrot soup, chicken-&-rice, and flan.

**MARIELA**.  No.

**JOSÉ**.  I want flan!

**MARIELA**.  José, you are dying of diabetes.

**JOSÉ**.  Fuck the Doctor. Fuck you. I want flan.

**MARIELA**.  First your insulin. Now.

**JOSÉ**.  If I get my flan.

**MARIELA**.  I'll see what I can do.

>   (**MARIELA** *has a small glass jar. She extracts insulin into the syringe. She gives* **JOSÉ** *his shot; he flinches.)*

**JOSÉ**.  You like doing that, don't you?

**MARIELA**.  Helping you?

**JOSÉ**.  Hurting me.

**MARIELA.** Helping...hurting...no difference sometimes.

**JOSÉ.** Mariela?

**MARIELA.** What?

**JOSÉ.** You think Blanca will come?

(**MARIELA** *kisses his forehead.*)

**MARIELA.** Clean the latrine.

**JOSÉ.** What?

**MARIELA.** That's what I choose to do. (**MARIELA** *exits.*)

(**OLIVA**'s *portrait.*)

**OLIVA.** When I was a girl, my mother said, "You are a lady, destined for fine things." I had dresses of silk. I knew how to waltz. I dreamt of my large house – of an elegant husband – of children of my own. Now, I live in a dark dress at the edge of the world in a parched house that my brother owns. Forever unmarried. Forever childless. My hands are empty. My heart is idle. I have nothing of my own.

(*Lights shift.*)

**MARIELA.** José wants flan.

**OLIVA.** Mariela, we can't give him that! The doctor said we can't...The sugar alone will...

**MARIELA.** He wants flan.

**OLIVA.** His blood will turn to molasses. He can't have it.

**MARIELA.** Ah, so this is your decision.

**OLIVA.** He's my baby brother.

**MARIELA.** Then you tell the baby you aren't going to serve him.

**OLIVA**. *(Pause.)* Maybe, I'll just take him a little slice.

**MARIELA**. Fine.

**OLIVA**. Do you think Blanca will come home this time?

**MARIELA**. I sent her a telegram. I think she will come.

**OLIVA**. That's good. It's been too long. A daughter should be with her father when he is sick. Sometimes I look at José and I think...miracles can happen.

**MARIELA**. Oliva, the doctor told us José will be dead by spring.

**OLIVA**. Why are you so cruel?

**MARIELA**. I'm not cruel. I am preparing you for what will happen.

**OLIVA**. *(Pause.)* What will become of me when he dies?

**MARIELA**. Do you think I'll send you away after José is gone?

**OLIVA**. I have nowhere to go!

**MARIELA**. Nowhere is here, Oliva. And you can always stay here with me.

> (**OLIVA** *is touched...she makes a movement towards* **MARIELA** *but* **MARIELA** *deflects it, turning to do something.)*

**OLIVA**. When do you think Blanca will come?

**MARIELA**. Tonight. Tomorrow morning at the latest.

**OLIVA**. It is right for her to be here. You, know with tomorrow being what it is.

**MARIELA**. Carlos' eighteenth birthday.

**OLIVA**. We should honor him.

**MARIELA**. Oliva –

**OLIVA.** Light a candle. Pray. Together.

**MARIELA.** We can't...

**OLIVA.** Mariela –

**MARIELA.** I need to prepare Blanca's room.

**OLIVA.** All right.

**MARIELA.** We need to clean it and place fresh linens on her bed.

**OLIVA.** Some people in town, they say they've seen him.

**MARIELA.** Seen who?

**OLIVA.** Carlos.

**MARIELA.** *(Pause.)* Carlos is dead, Oli.

**OLIVA.** I know. But people in town tell stories. About the fire.

**MARIELA.** The fire.

**OLIVA.** And that they see a little boy running in the desert.

**MARIELA.** People always see strange things in the desert.

**OLIVA.** People say the running boy is Carlos.

**MARIELA.** Have you seen him?

**OLIVA.** No. Of course not. Have you?

**MARIELA.** I am going to clean and rearrange Blanca's room. End of ridiculous conversation.

**OLIVA.** That poor, sweet, troubled child.

(**MARIELA** *glares at her. Beat.*)

So you'll clean her bedroom.

**MARIELA.** Yes, and you will take dinner to José. Give him the flan first. It will make him happy.

(**OLIVA** *exits singing a sad song about happiness.*\*)

**MARIELA.**  My poor Carlos.

(*Flashback. Music*\*. *Mexico City, years ago. We hear* **JOSÉ** *call out from the past: "Mariela" then* **JOSÉ** *strides in, young and strong.*)

**JOSÉ**.  Mariela! Our party is a roaring success! That toad Diego Rivera can't keep his eyes off you!

**MARIELA.**  (*Laughs.*) Shhh! Our guests, they'll hear you!

**JOSÉ.**  Can you believe it, all these people! Where's the cognac? I want to give them all our good cognac.

**MARIELA.**  I have coffee on the fire. Frida asked for coffee.

**JOSÉ.**  Siqueiros wants cognac.

**MARIELA.**  He's pretty drunk already. Who's the girl on his lap?

**JOSÉ**.  She's that Modotti girl. Italian. From the United States. She is screwing that skinny American photographer over there.

**MARIELA.**  I asked who she is.

**JOSÉ.**  She is who she sleeps with.

**MARIELA.**  (*Wraps herself around* **JOSÉ**.) Does that make me you?

**JOSÉ.**  You're too beautiful to be me.

**MARIELA.**  (*Kisses him.*) Not in the dark.

---

\* A license to produce *Mariela in the Desert* does not include a performance license for any third-party or copyrighted music. Licensees should create an original composition or use music in the public domain. For further information, please see the Music and Third-Party Materials Use Note on page iii.

**JOSÉ.** Do you know how many famous painters are in that room?

**MARIELA.** They're our friends.

**JOSÉ.** Our famous friends! If I had had connections to this type of people when I was your age, do you know how great my career would be? Every gallery in Mexico, France, and the United States would be selling my paintings. I would be a Presidential Medal winner already.

**MARIELA.** You are a great artist. It will happen for you, José.

**JOSÉ.** Oh yes it will. Now that we know these people…

**MARIELA.** Shh.

**JOSÉ.** What?

**MARIELA.** I thought Carlos was crying. Again.

**JOSÉ.** It's just Rufino singing.

**MARIELA.** I think it's the baby.

**JOSÉ.** Blanca is sleeping and the baby is fine. Look at me. We were talking, Diego and I. About how bourgeois Mexico City is. About how important it is for all of us to get together. To help each other. We should move out of Mexico City. Invite our friends, our comrades. To inspire each other and make better art. We should build a commune.

**MARIELA.** Build a commune? Where?

**JOSÉ.** We could build a ranch. Or buy one. Put my family money to good use. Up north. In the desert.

**MARIELA.** The desert is a stark place, José.

**JOSÉ.** *(Discovery.)* The desert is God's canvas.

**MARIELA.** But the children –

**JOSÉ.** – Will love it! The desert – its emptiness – will demand to be filled with color, with art, with our vision of a better world. The desert will define us as artists, as a community, as a movement! We will be the talented artistic couple that finally inspired beauty in the art of Frida, Rufino, Siqueiros, even Diego. Do you know what this will do for my painting career? Everyone will want to come and be part of it.

**MARIELA.** As long as we feed them –

**JOSÉ.** Diego wants you pose for him.

**MARIELA.** Me? Why?

**JOSÉ.** Because you are beautiful. He asked me if you would.

**MARIELA.** He's married too.

**JOSÉ.** Frida. She's spooky.

**MARIELA.** She's tiny.

**JOSÉ.** She's barren, you know.

**MARIELA.** José, please, she's our guest.

**JOSÉ.** For a famous man, you'd think he'd smell better. He's an ugly son of a bitch. We're the same age, practically, him and me. I hate his latest mural. The one with the workers with the strange square fists. So primitive and dark.

**MARIELA.** He's angry.

**JOSÉ.** So what? I'm angry! His brush is too heavy.

**MARIELA.** I like the coarseness.

**JOSÉ.** You would.

**MARIELA.** It's vivid and raw. The texture resembles the weave of a basket. And the blood has the feel of clay, the skin the roughness of the earth

**JOSÉ.** All Diego does is make an ugly world uglier. This angry new " movement" is just artists farting in the face of God. But at our ranch, all our friends, even Diego will find the right inspiration and come back to beauty. It's called fine arts, for Christ's Sake! You shouldn't ever treat paint like mortar. Will you pose for him?

**MARIELA**. I don't know.

**JOSÉ**. Listen to me. El cabrón says you have a certain "vulnerable and potent aura." He wants to see you naked! It will drive him crazy. I love it. I love the idea of Rivera wanting something that only I can have.

**MARIELA**. *(Pause.)* I will let him paint me, if he lets me paint him.

**JOSÉ**. What?

**MARIELA**. If he wants me to pose naked for him, then he must pose naked for me.

**JOSÉ**. No! You are a married woman.

**MARIELA**. So is Frida.

**JOSÉ**. Frida is not my wife.

**MARIELA**. So as your wife, I am allowed to pose nude for Diego, but Diego is not allowed to pose nude for me?

**JOSÉ**. That's not what I said.

**MARIELA**. He will be my model. Show him my work!

**JOSÉ**. I did show it to him.

**MARIELA**. Which painting did you show him? Did you show him *The Bent Woman*?

**JOSÉ**. *(Beat.)* I did.

**MARIELA**. And what did he say? *(Beat.)* Tell me. What did he say?

**JOSÉ**. *(Beat.)* He said he hopes you are a better lover than you are a painter.

　　　　*(Pause.)*

**MARIELA**. And what did you say? *(Beat.)* Do you think I'm a better lover than an artist?

**JOSÉ.**     Diego is famous. You are still young and inexperienced. But you have talent. Think of what you could learn if Diego and Frida and Siqueiros would come work with us in our commune. So, what should I tell him?

**MARIELA.**  Tell your friend Diego, that my deal still stands. If he wants to paint me, I have to paint him.

**JOSÉ.**  Dammit. I ask for so little and you say "No."

**MARIELA.**  I didn't say "No," I said –

**JOSÉ.**  You are cruel. You like to string out my intestines and chew on them. Why can't you just –

**MARIELA.**  José, I am going to check on Blanca and the baby.

**JOSÉ.**  Diego could help my career. Don't you want me to be successful?

**MARIELA.**  José, of course I do –

*(The baby starts to cry, loudly.)*

Carlos is crying. You know how agitated he gets...

**JOSÉ.**  *(Grabs her arm or blocks her.)* You have to help me, Mari.

**MARIELA.**  Fine. I'll pose for Diego.

**JOSÉ.**  Naked?

**MARIELA.**  Anything you want! I need to get the baby.

**JOSÉ.**  So, you will you help me?

**MARIELA.**  I'll help you.

**JOSÉ.**  *(Embraces her.)* Thank you. Where is the cognac?

*(**JOSÉ** exits. **MARIELA** turns to get **CARLOS**.)*

**MARIELA.**  Carlos! *(Beat. Realizes **CARLOS** is gone. Shift in light.)* Carlos, my poor baby boy.

(**OLIVA** *runs in. It's the present again.*)

**OLIVA**. JOSÉ! Stop it!

**JOSÉ**. Goddamn bunch of assassins each and every one of you.

**OLIVA**. José, you shouldn't swear like that...

(**JOSÉ** *hurls a plate at her.*)

**JOSÉ**. Den of murderers, both of you!

**MARIELA**. Oliva, get out now.

**OLIVA**. Calm down, José.

**MARIELA**. Oliva get out! José, calm down.

**OLIVA**. This excitement is not good for you.

**JOSÉ**. Are you trying to kill me?

**OLIVA**. The flan was her idea.

**JOSÉ**. No! The flan was my idea.

**OLIVA**. I'm sorry.

(**OLIVA** *leaves the room.*)

**MARIELA**. Not so loud.

**JOSÉ**. The flan could kill me. And you send it...send it with my sister! You can't even do your own dirty work.

**MARIELA**. I was cleaning the latrine! Besides, you insisted on it. It was a small sliver.

**JOSÉ**. A man shouldn't get everything he wants.

**MARIELA**. I was trying to be kind.

**JOSÉ**. Killing me is not kindness!!! Even if it makes me happy.

**MARIELA**. Calm down.

**JOSÉ.** I'm dying, Mariela. My fingers, my cheeks, my toes. I'm dying bit by bit. Everything hurts.

**MARIELA.** *(Soothes him.)* I know. *(Beat.)* Did you have anything to eat?

**JOSÉ.** The flan. I tasted it.

**MARIELA.** Was it good?

**JOSÉ.** It was sweet. Very sweet. Creamy. *(Beat.)* Why does it have to be so sweet?

I couldn't stop, it tasted so sweet. I don't want to stop!

**MARIELA.** José, please, let me take you back to your room.

**JOSÉ.** I'm so thirsty.

**MARIELA.** Do you need some water?

**JOSÉ.** I'm always thirsty.

**MARIELA.** We live in a dry desert.

> *(She gives him a drink.)*

**JOSÉ.** When will Blanca come back? I miss her so much.

**MARIELA.** She could be here any moment.

**JOSÉ.** Good. I miss her so much.

**MARIELA.** Let me help you.

**JOSÉ.** Don't help me!

**MARIELA.** Fine! Sleep!

> *(**MARIELA** stoops to pick the broken plate. She gets the broom and sweeps. **OLIVA** just talks.)*

**OLIVA.** He's gone to bed?

**MARIELA.** Yes. What a mess.

**OLIVA.** I've never seen him like this.

**MARIELA.** I know.

**OLIVA.**  The older and sicker he gets, the more he becomes like a child.

**MARIELA.**  I know.

**OLIVA.**  You know, when José was a boy, he could climb a tree faster than a cat. He could eat half a cow for lunch. He could ride a horse without stirrups. Now, he can do none of these things.

**MARIELA.**  I know.

**OLIVA.**  I feel terrible. I want to help.

**MARIELA.**  You feeling terrible helps, immensely.

**OLIVA.**  Another of my mother's good plates, gone!

**MARIELA.**  I never cared for the pattern.

**OLIVA.**  These are beautiful. When I was a girl, I thought they would be mine.

**MARIELA.**  Well, it's fortunate then, that you live here with us and get to use them everyday.

**OLIVA.**  Yes. These plates desperately needed a good cook.

**MARIELA.**  How true, Oliva.

**OLIVA.**  He just went wild.

**MARIELA.**  I know.

**OLIVA.**  He stabbed me with a fork.

**MARIELA.**  Just now?

**OLIVA.**  On the hand. Surprised the Spirit out of me.

**MARIELA.**  Let me see. Oli, stop what you're doing. Come, we need to clean this.

**OLIVA.**  I'll have to go to the well. We are out of water.

**MARIELA.**  No, we need to put some alcohol on it.

**OLIVA.** He stabbed me like I was a piece of pork. It happened so fast, it didn't even hurt.

(**MARIELA** *applies alcohol.*)

Ay, Holy Mother of Jesus! That stings!

**MARIELA.** Hold it tight.

**OLIVA.** He got me deep.

**MARIELA.** That's his way.

**OLIVA.** He's strong for a...

**MARIELA.** For a dying man. Yes, in some ways, I guess he is.

**OLIVA.** You know, the priest told me, he could come.

**MARIELA.** And how does the priest know about José?

**OLIVA.** Maybe someone told him.

**MARIELA.** Does everyone in town know?

**OLIVA.** Well the Priest, the Doctor and his wife and children and the maid and her neighbors and – yes. Everybody.

**MARIELA.** Already? What are the people saying?

**OLIVA.** How am I supposed to know? I mean, I'm here, not there and they say whatever they –

(**MARIELA** *looks at her.*)

Cursed.

**MARIELA.** Cursed.

**OLIVA.** Cursed. They say God closes his eyes whenever He looks over here.

**MARIELA.** Ignored even by God.

**OLIVA.** I think the priest needs to come.

**MARIELA.** No.

**OLIVA.** José wants absolution.

**MARIELA**.  José wants attention. *(Beat.)* You will have to wash the wound again, later.

**OLIVA**.  You should let God take care of you.

**MARIELA**.  I prefer somebody more reliable.

> (**OLIVA** *withdraws her arm from* **MARIELA***'s grip.*)

Don't look at me like that, Oli.

**OLIVA**.  I pray for you every night. God wants to love you. He does. And I want to also.

**MARIELA**.  *(Passionately. Painting a picture with words.)* When I was twelve years old, my parents were dragged off to jail for attending a secret Roman Catholic Mass. They were Cristeros and the government was really coming down on the Church. Our town priest, fearing for his life, ran to the United States. My mother was released after a few weeks, but my father was gone for over a year. He was tortured, you know. And I was so proud that my father took a longer sentence instead of denying his faith. "The Church is my only governor. I will pray no matter what the law says," he said that in his trial.

**OLIVA**.  Your father?

**MARIELA**.  My grandmother, my mother, and I prayed for my father's release relentlessly, with no Church, no congregation, no confession. We prayed. In the movie theater. Watching *King Kong*, we got on our knees and prayed. To God, to the Virgin, the saints, the apostles.

**OLIVA**.  And did your father come back?

**MARIELA**.  Yes, and we felt blessed…until he ran off with the priest's maid a month later.

**OLIVA**.  That's not God's fault!

**MARIELA**.  It all has very little to do with God, doesn't it?

**OLIVA.** *(Pause.)* I didn't know that about you.

**MARIELA.** Because it isn't true.

**OLIVA.** You lied to me?

**MARIELA.** We are not cursed, Oliva. People make their own misery. I told you a story to make you forget the pain in your hand.

> (**MARIELA** *picks up a dark piece of cloth and starts to cover the lone slit painting.*)

**OLIVA.** What are you doing?

**MARIELA.** I'm covering the painting.

**OLIVA.** It's become an awful picture. Why don't we just put it away?

**MARIELA.** It's a masterpiece. José wants it up.

**OLIVA.** It's so hard to look at.

**MARIELA.** We have to learn to live with what we do.

**OLIVA.** So why cover it tonight?

**MARIELA.** Because Blanca is coming. *(A rustle.)* Do you hear something?

**OLIVA.** Do you?

**MARIELA.** It must be the desert wind.

> *(Pause, The wind blows. An odd eerie quiet.)*

**OLIVA.** Will you sleep tonight?

**MARIELA.** I'll sit next to José's door. In case he needs me.

**OLIVA.** You should lie in your bed.

**MARIELA.** I have the rest of my life to do that. For now, I'll sit on a chair outside José's room.

**OLIVA.** That's good. If you want, I can knit and sit vigil too.

**MARIELA.**  Thank you, but I prefer being good by myself.

(**OLIVA** *exits.* **MARIELA** *sits.*)

(**BLANCA**'s *portrait.*)

**BLANCA.**  When I first left the desert, I was fifteen years old. My father's studio had burned to the ground; my little brother's body in the ashes of the fire. I wanted to hold on to this place like a blanket. But as the car pulled away and my parents faded in the distance, I discovered I wanted to run. Run as far away as I could.

Tonight, I return to the desert. My father is dead. The wind blows. It welcomes. It warns. The doorknob is cold and firm in my hand. I seem so different but, inside, I am unchanged. I am as lost as I have ever been. I am home.

(**BLANCA** *steps in. Light change.*)

**MARIELA.**  You came.

**BLANCA.**  Mami, how can my Papi be dead?

**MARIELA.**  Oh, Blanquita.

(**MARIELA** *steps towards* **BLANCA** *but* **OLIVA** *enters.* **BLANCA** *falls into her aunt's arms.*)

**BLANCA.**  Oli!

**OLIVA.**  Blanquita. I've missed you so much. You've grown so much.

**BLANCA.**  I know.

**OLIVA.**  You are so beautiful.

**BLANCA.**  Oli, my poor Papi!

**OLIVA.**  I know. So much suffering.

**BLANCA.**  I can't believe Papi is dead!

**OLIVA.** Dead? (**OLIVA** *shoots* **MARIELA** *a look.*)

**MARIELA.** Blanca, who is that man outside?

**OLIVA.** A Man? Here? Where?

**MARIELA.** Sitting in that car. Blanca, why is the driver not leaving?

**BLANCA.** The man in the car is with me.

(*Beat.* **MARIELA** *and* **OLIVA** *share a look.*)

**OLIVA.** What do you mean "with you?"

**BLANCA.** His name is Adam... Adam Lovitz. He is a professor from the United States. He teaches Art History at the University.

**OLIVA.** You traveled alone through this desert with an American Man?

**MARIELA.** An American Man that teaches Art History?

**OLIVA.** God have mercy.

**BLANCA.** Oliva, please, it's 1951. (*Beat.*) Adam is a professor and highly respected in his field. He has PhD from Columbia University. He is currently writing a book on Mexican Expressionism.

**OLIVA.** Should we invite him in?

**MARIELA.** He looks a little old for you. Are you sleeping with him?

**OLIVA.** Mariela!

**BLANCA.** There's less of an age difference between us than Papi and you.

**OLIVA.** Blanca! Oh no! Jesus in Heaven. Blanca, men say things...to make you do things. One humid night with the wrong man, and my life was never –

**MARIELA.** Oli, this isn't your ancient history. Please let Blanca and me have a moment together, alone.

**OLIVA**. *(Kisses* **BLANCA**.*)* I'll be in my room praying if you need me, Blanquita.

*(***OLIVA*** exits.)*

**MARIELA**. You know, this house has been so empty since you left. So empty.

*(***BLANCA*** cries.* **MARIELA** *strokes her hair.)*

**BLANCA**. I can't believe Papi is gone. I miss my Papi so much.

**MARIELA**. Shhh. My baby. It's not so bad, not so bad. It's going to be all right.

**BLANCA**. What do you mean?

**MARIELA**. Things aren't as bad as you think.

**BLANCA**. What?

**MARIELA**. *(Beat.)* You shouldn't believe everything you read.

**BLANCA**. *(Pause.)* Oh God. *(Beat.)* He's not dead, is he?

**MARIELA**. Well –

**BLANCA**. He's not dead! Papi is not dead!

**MARIELA**. *(Pause.)* He's sick.

**BLANCA**. He's been sick since Carlos died. Mami, you lied to me.

**MARIELA**. Blanca, your father is dying.

**BLANCA**. Does Oliva know?

**MARIELA**. That he's sick? Of course.

**BLANCA**. About the telegram? You send this God forsaken note. I went crazy. You...you make me just drop everything. What is wrong with you?

**MARIELA**. What is wrong with you?

**BLANCA**. What?

**MARIELA.** This is the only way to get you to come home.

**BLANCA.** That's not true.

**MARIELA.** You're here, aren't you?

**BLANCA.** But to say he is "dead"...

**MARIELA.** You need to see you father before he dies.

(**BLANCA** *really looks at* **MARIELA.**)

**BLANCA.** He's really dying?

**MARIELA.** Yes.

**BLANCA.** How long does he have?

**MARIELA.** A few weeks. Maybe a couple months.

His blood is slow and thick. His eyesight is blurring. And he had three toes amputated last month.

**BLANCA.** What? Where?

**MARIELA.** On his foot, dear.

**BLANCA.** At what hospital?

**MARIELA.** The doctor comes.

**BLANCA.** Papi should be in a hospital.

**MARIELA.** Your father is convinced he's sick enough to die, but not sick enough to go to a hospital.

**BLANCA.** I want to see him.

**MARIELA.** I'll take you.

**BLANCA.** No, I want to see him by myself, with my own eyes. Alone.

**MARIELA.** We brought a bed and a wheelchair down to the library.

**BLANCA.** He needs a wheelchair?

**MARIELA.** You really should come home more often.

*(***BLANCA*** *runs out towards the study.)*

**BLANCA.**  Papi!

**MARIELA.**  Don't upset him. Tell him you are married.

**BLANCA.**  Papi wouldn't want me to lie to him.

**MARIELA.**  About this, believe me, he would.

*(***BLANCA*** *exits.)*

*(Flashback: We hear "MAMI MAMI!" Then* ***CARLOS*** *races in.)*

**CARLOS.**  Please Mami! Kill it! Kill it! A scorpion!

*(***MARIELA*** *grabs a broom.)*

**MARIELA.**  Ahh! There it goes. Stay away from it! Carlos, stop squealing! This is dangerous!

*(***BLANCA*** *enters.)*

**BLANCA.**  Ay! A scorpion, Mami! It's running!!

**CARLOS.**  Ohhh, here it comes!!!

**MARIELA.**  It's so fast.

**BLANCA.**  Oooh! Let me do it!

**MARIELA.**  NO! Get away! And feet off the floor.

*(The children giddily jump on the furniture.* ***JOSÉ*** *enters.)*

**JOSÉ.**  What's going on here?

**BLANCA & CARLOS.**  *(Excited.)* Papi, it's a scorpion!

**CARLOS.**  *(Happy.)* Save me!

**JOSÉ.**  Save you? What about me?

*(***JOSÉ*** *jumps on the furniture to the children's delight. They all squeal.)*

**MARIELA.** *(Laughs.)* José!

**JOSÉ.** Watch out, Mariela, there it goes!

> *(Excited giggles.)*

**CARLOS.** Mami, get it! Get it!

**BLANCA.** It's running. It's running! That way!

**MARIELA.** Where? Ah!

**JOSÉ.** She's got it cornered!

**MARIELA.** Ah-ha! There!

> *(Boom.* **MARIELA** *lowers the broom and kills it.)*

**ALL.** *(Sobering sound.)* Ohhh.

**MARIELA.** Children, and that includes you José, this is why you have to wear shoes all the time... All the time. The next time I catch you not wearing shoes –

**CARLOS.** He's dead. He was running and running and now he's just dead.

**BLANCA.** Killed.

**MARIELA.** *(Beat.)* I was protecting you. All of you.

> *(***JOSÉ*** and the children go inspect the dead bug.)*

**BLANCA.** Mami, you killed a baby scorpion!

**JOSÉ.** *(Being silly and dramatic.)* Mariela, how could you? I would never hurt a fly!

**MARIELA.** *(Cuts through the noise.)* When I was twelve years old, I saw a big fat bull die in seconds. The bull bellowed, frothed at the mouth and then crumpled to the ground in one fell swoop. Killed by a baby scorpion. You see, the young ones are the most dangerous. They can't control their poison.

*(Solemn appreciation for the power of the bug.)*

**BLANCA.** Why did we have to move here? It's so hot and dry and scary bugs. I want to go back to Mexico City.

**MARIELA.** We live here now.

**BLANCA.** Why?

**JOSÉ.** It's so open and beautiful here. The desert is God's Canvas. Do you know how many children would love to live on a ranch in the desert?

**BLANCA.** No.

**JOSÉ.** We are building a community. Your mother and I will fill this vastness with our art.

**MARIELA.** José, I haven't painted since we got here.

**JOSÉ.** You will. Once we get settled in...find our footing...we will water this desert with our paint. A masterpiece will come out of this house...out of that old barn out there!

**CARLOS.** The scorpion is so still.

**BLANCA.** The scorpion is so dead.

**JOSÉ.** *(Picks it up.)* It's fine. I'm doing a burial at sea. Those wishing to clean their conscience can follow me to the latrine.

**MARIELA.** Please don't waste water on that thing.

**CARLOS.** Noooo.

*(**JOSÉ** and **MARIELA** look at each other.)*

**BLANCA.** Carlos, don't do that.

**CARLOS.** The scorpion is so still. He's so still. He's so still.

**BLANCA.** Mami, he's doing it again.

**JOSÉ.** Carlos –

**CARLOS.** So still. So still.

**MARIELA**. Carlos, please stop.

> (**CARLOS** *is hurting himself, hitting his head against the wall, pulling his hair.*)

**BLANCA**. Mami –

**MARIELA**. José, get Blanca out of here. Take her to the barn.

**JOSÉ**. Come, m'ija.

> (**JOSÉ** *and* **BLANCA** *exit.*)

> (**CARLOS** *is suffering.*)

**CARLOS**. So still.

> (**MARIELA** *envelops him.*)

**MARIELA**. Carlos, please don't do that. You will hurt yourself.

**CARLOS**. Mami he was running. And then he was so still.

**MARIELA**. Carlos, please calm down.

**CARLOS**. I can't.

**MARIELA**. Yes you can. Bite your lip. Like me.

**CARLOS**. To keep the scream inside?

**MARIELA**. Yes. Hold that scream inside…until it's gone. Shh.

> (**CARLOS** *continues to quietly bite his lip and sniff and cry.*)

Good boy. Now try to stop crying.

> (**JOSÉ** *looks in.* **MARIELA** *waves him away.*)

**CARLOS**. *(Stops. Serious.)* But how do you bite your eyelids?

> (**MARIELA** *laughs and hugs him.*)

**MARIELA**. You can't bite your eyelids, silly.

> (**BLANCA** *comes in, stands far away, watching her* **MARIELA** *hug* **CARLOS**.)

**CARLOS.** What was that?

**MARIELA.** It's just the desert wind.

> *(She kisses him and starts to sing him a lullaby.\*)*

**CARLOS.** So tired.

> *(**CARLOS** walks off stage. **MARIELA** turns and sees **BLANCA** standing alone, confused, and hurt. **BLANCA** looks at **MARIELA** and runs off.)*
>
> *(End of flashback.)*
>
> *(**ADAM** enters. **ADAM**'s portrait.)*

**ADAM.** It's cold in the desert. I am foreigner in a foreign land, uninvited and unexpected. I like the cold. I like the dry feel of this vast indifferent land. I am here for the funeral of a famous Mexican artist, an artist whose paintings have all but disappeared. I am not here for him, but for Blanca. *(Beat.)* I am an outsider: I am at home where I do not belong.

> *(Light shift.)*

**MARIELA.** You must be the American Professor. I'm sorry, we both forgot all about you. Come in.

**ADAM.** I just wanted to give you and Blanca a moment.

**MARIELA.** Wise of you, I'm Mariela Salvatierra.

**ADAM.** I'm Adam Lovitz, Señora Salvatierra.

**MARIELA.** You can call me Mariela if you like, seeing that we are so close in age.

---

\* A license to produce *Mariela in the Desert* does not include a performance license for any third-party or copyrighted music. Licensees should create an original composition or use music in the public domain. For further information, please see the Music and Third-Party Materials Use Note on page iii.

**ADAM.** I'm sorry for your loss.

**MARIELA.** Which one?

**ADAM.** Excuse me?

**MARIELA.** Would you like something to drink?

**ADAM.** Please, I don't want to be any trouble.

**MARIELA.** So is that yes or no?

**ADAM.** Excuse me?

**MARIELA.** To the drink.

**ADAM.** No, thank you. Where's Blanca?

**MARIELA.** She's in there with her Father. Poor thing. Long trip?

**ADAM.** Yes. We flew. We drove. The roads are quite...uneven.

**MARIELA.** You speak our language rather well for an American.

**ADAM.** Thank you. I started teaching myself in middle school after I discovered a comic book about Pancho Villa in Spanish. The pictures were so vivid, I just had to know what they were saying.

**MARIELA.** Thank you for bringing my girl.

**ADAM.** Blanca is very upset.

**MARIELA.** Losing a parent is never easy, is it?

**ADAM.** Mine are still alive.

**MARIELA.** We don't know very much about you, except that you're older than my daughter and you teach art.

**ADAM.** I teach Art History.

**MARIELA.** And what brought you to Mexico?

**ADAM.** I'm teaching a course in Mexico City at the University.

"National Identity in Modern Mexican Expressionism."

**MARIELA.** An American teaching us about our art?

**ADAM.** An outside perspective can be helpful sometimes.

**MARIELA.** Why aren't you teaching in a fancy university in the United States of America?

**ADAM.** Extended sabbatical. *(Pause.)* Philosophical differences.

**MARIELA.** Such as?

**ADAM.** Well, you see, Señora Salvatierra –

**MARIELA.** Mariela –

**ADAM.** Currently, there is an obsession in the United States with gestural abstraction that perplexes me. Critics, academics, collectors are all slobbering over the work of artists like Jackson Pollock. They are so excited about his chaotic process, his splish-splash of color, that they do not see he is a man who is communicating nothing. On the other hand, here, Mexican Expressionism gets at the core of why I think art needs to exist.

**MARIELA.** Ah! And why does art need to exist, Professor?

**ADAM.** Because at its core...art is about communication, a vital human conversation, a dangerous dialogue between the artist and the viewer.

**MARIELA.** So you were fired.

**ADAM.** Pollock is not abstract, he is random. His work is non-political, impersonal, safe. He throws paint on a canvas. None of his paintings present his point of view. Frida Kahlo slashes open her beating heart and lets it bleed: "This" she paints "is how it feels to love a man more than he loves you." We cannot ignore the brutal truth behind her statement. What do I learn about Pollock when I look at his work? Nothing.

**MARIELA.** But some would argue of his paintings are beautiful. The vivid colors, the curve of the paint. The energy of the drops.

**ADAM.**  Pollock's art is tasteful but hollow. He gives nothing of himself. It is a one sided conversation.

**MARIELA.**  My husband used to say art should be about beauty.

**ADAM.**  Art should be about truth *(Beat.)* and there is always something beautiful about the truth...no matter how ugly that truth may be. *(Beat.)* I was hoping to meet your husband... You know I am writing a chapter about him in my book.

*(Pause. Points to the lone covered painting.)* Is that one his?

**MARIELA.**  It's *The Blue Barn*.

**ADAM.**  *The Blue Barn. The Blue Barn*? That piece was revolutionary in terms of Salvatierra's work, exposing a deeper, more personal vision. That painting promised an exciting new direction in Mexican Expressionism. It's here? Here? I thought it was destroyed in the fire when the studio burned down. *The Blue Barn*?! A green little boy standing in the window.

**MARIELA.**  My son, Carlos. Yes.

**ADAM.**  And an orange bird flying over a well?

**MARIEA.**  Blanca.

**ADAM.**  Blanca?! Of course. *The Blue Barn* –

**MARIELA.**  "The Crown jewel of Salvatierra's work."

**ADAM.**  It's the only Presidential Prize Winner not hanging at the National Museum of Fine Arts.

**MARIELA.**  Because it's here. Covered with the heavy black shroud of mourning.

(**ADAM** *stops. Pause.*)

**ADAM.**  I'm sorry. This house is grieving.

**MARIELA.**  In so many ways.

**ADAM.** *(Pause.)* It's so cold at night in the desert.

**MARIELA.** Especially in the winter. So come professor. Make yourself at home. Let's fill this room with stuffy hot air and tell me, how you met my daughter.

**ADAM.** Blanca sat first row in my seminar. She fixed her eyes on me but refused to take notes; she never contributed to the discussion. While all the other students would clamor to talk to me after class, Blanca would disappear the second my lecture ended. She showed up for every exam, politely folded her hands on her lap, and then would hand in a blank sheet. She was the first student to ever flunk my class.

**MARIELA.** My daughter failed?

**ADAM.** When she showed up for the next semester, I asked her why she was wasting both our time, taking the course again. She looked me straight in the eye and said she wanted to give me a second chance to get it right. Then she handed me a box of her drawings and paintings.

**MARIELA.** She's still painting.

**ADAM.** Blanca uses lots of color. Explosive shapes. Broad strokes and then exquisite detail. To experience a vision like hers is like being caught in an earthquake. Her paintings carve out a jagged, uncomfortable, and fascinating new terrain in Mexican Expressionism.

**MARIELA.** Really?

**ADAM.** Blanca's paintings were recently part of an exhibit in Mexico City. Her series of nudes stole the show. Sold several pieces for three thousand pesos each.

**MARIELA.** That much?

**ADAM.** Blanca is making a name for herself as an artist. Your daughter has inherited your husband's talent.

**MARIELA.** Please don't say that.

**ADAM.** Why not?

**MARIELA.** Because talent is a burden.

(Pause.)

**ADAM.** I apologize. I didn't mean to upset you.

**MARIELA.** Is Blanca a better artist than my husband?

**ADAM.** That's not for me to say.

**MARIELA.** You are an art history professor. You are the ones who decide who's immortalized and who's forgotten.

**ADAM.** Señora Salvatierra, your husband has just died.

**MARIELA.** And you still haven't answered my question. Is Blanca better?

**ADAM.** If Blanca can continue this exciting trend –

**MARIELA.** Professor Lovitz, there is a big difference between talent and trend.

**ADAM.** Your daughter is talented. And I love her, I can assure you.

**MARIELA.** And let me assure you that does not assure me.

**ADAM.** I realize you don't know me.

**MARIELA.** Oh, but I do, professor. To the core.

**ADAM.** You have the wrong idea.

**MARIELA.** As if you would have any idea what is in my head at this moment.

**ADAM.** You see an American…a gringo standing between you and your daughter.

**MARIELA.** Is that what you think I see?

**ADAM.** Yes.

**MARIELA.** I see a thin, jagged cactus, a palo verde, green and tugging at the sky, while it's tawny roots suck every drop of rain hidden in the crusty dry soil. Yes, a young beautiful cactus. And you professor, are just a little prick, in her side.

**ADAM.** *(Beat.)* I don't think you like me.

**MARIELA.** Oh I like you, I just don't trust you.

**ADAM.** After the funeral, I'm taking Blanca back home.

**MARIELA.** But now you are in her Father's home. And he can't wait to meet you.

**ADAM.** Excuse me?

**MARIELA.** José would love to meet you, I'm sure.

**ADAM.** *(Beat.)* Isn't your husband dead?

**MARIELA.** No.

**ADAM.** But your telegram –

**MARIELA.** See that's the problem with writing chapters in art history books. You base everything on documents and research, never thinking that people may say or write things down that may be very important, very necessary, but not actually true. I wrote that telegram because Blanca needs to be here. *(Pause.)* And now we get to meet you as well.

**ADAM.** I think I'd like that drink now.

(**MARIELA** *serves him.*)

**MARIELA.** I think that's a good idea. Lovitz...what type of a name is that?

**ADAM.** I'm Jewish.

**MARIELA.** That's what I thought. I always felt I was Jewish, in a lapsed – Mexican Catholic sort of way.

*(There's a rustling in the shadows.)*

*(A wisp of moment, hope, fear.)*

Is something the matter?

**ADAM.** I thought I saw someone.

**MARIELA.** I hear the wind.

**ADAM.** I saw someone. Outside. In the shadows.

(**MARIELA** *gets up and peers into the shadows.*)

I thought I saw someone running.

**MARIELA.** Running?

**ADAM.** A young boy. Maybe. Yes.

**MARIELA.** Where was he?

**ADAM.** Out there I don't know. I think –

(*The wind blows again.*)

**MARIELA.** This desert is hot and quiet during the day...but it moans and slithers at night.

**ADAM.** Look. Listen.

(*Quiet. They listen. Rustling.* **OLIVA** *enters.*)

**MARIELA.** Oliva!

**OLIVA.** What did I do?

**MARIELA.** Is this the someone you saw? This is Oliva, Blanca's aunt. My husband's sister.

**OLIVA.** I was just outside getting sheets off the line.

**MARIELA.** Yes. I'm sure your were. Meet Professor Lovitz.

**OLIVA.** (*To* **MARIELA.**) He's very handsome.

**ADAM.** Thank you.

**OLIVA.** (*Surprised he understood her.*) Oh! And he speaks the language so well.

(**ADAM** *extends his hand.*)

**MARIELA.** Yes he does. He's also American, Jewish, possibly a socialist and definitely Blanca's lover.

**OLIVA**. Oh dear God.

**MARIELA**. Now shake his hand.

**OLIVA**. *(Shakes his hand.)* "Let the sin of thine heart be cleansed by my hand." First Corinthians, I think.

**ADAM**. Thank you, I think.

**MARIELA**. Oliva hopes that one day God will keep us company in our utter isolation.

**OLIVA**. She needs me. They all need me.

(**BLANCA** *enters.*)

**BLANCA**. Mami, what is happening here?

**MARIELA**. Introductions.

**OLIVA**. Blanca, linda, –

**BLANCA**. Don't pretend you didn't know, Oli.

**OLIVA**. About what?

**BLANCA**. My father! The telegram. You're supposed to be looking out for me.

**MARIELA**. I'm your mother.

**BLANCA**. Exactly. Adam, you won't believe this but...

**ADAM**. Your father is alive.

**BLANCA**. She told you?

**OLIVA**. I'm innocent. I never knew he was supposed to be dead.

**BLANCA**. Really, well, then why would you cover the painting, Oli?

**OLIVA**. You were coming!

**BLANCA**. Papi is fine. He is alive and vibrant and as sweet as ever!

**MARIELA**. He's dying.

**ADAM.** Perhaps you could have thought of another way to persuade Blanca to come home.

**BLANCA.** Yes.

**MARIELA.** Really, I am very sorry that it all came to this. One shouldn't have to persuade a daughter to act like a daughter.

**BLANCA.** That's enough!

**MARIELA.** Especially one as loved as Blanca.

**BLANCA.** This charade has gone too far.

       (**BLANCA** *pulls the shroud off the painting.*)

No!

**ADAM.** Oh my God.

**BLANCA.** What happened?

**ADAM.** Oh my God. *(Pause.)* Salvatierra's masterpiece.

**BLANCA.** How is this possible? When did this happen?

**ADAM.** Who did this? Who stabbed this painting?

       *(Silence.)*

**MARIELA.** José.

**BLANCA.** When?

**MARIELA.** Two days ago. That's when I knew he really is dying.

**BLANCA.** Poor Papi. We have to fix it.

**OLIVA.** I can't look at it.

**ADAM.** The gash is like a wound. It's almost intrinsic to the painting. The swirls of broken paint, the bleeding color. A vital honest cry of pain *(Beat.) The Blue Barn* is beautiful, even damaged.

**BLANCA.** No. It needs to be restored.

**MARIELA.** I don't think your father would like that.

**BLANCA.** I can convince him.

**MARIELA.** Your father must have been happy to see you.

**BLANCA.** He danced with happiness.

**MARIELA.** Danced! You should have come sooner.

**BLANCA.** He wants flan.

**MARIELA.** It makes him sick.

**OLIVA.** The Doctor said –

**BLANCA.** Dr. Gomez is a quack. You said so yourself.

**OLIVA.** That quack saved your life. *(To* **ADAM.***)* She fell in the well.

**BLANCA.** I already told Adam that story.

**MARIELA.** Quite inspired, really, don't you think, how Blanca managed to almost drown in the desert.

**BLANCA.** It was an accident.

**MARIELA.** Dancing on the edge of a well? That was a plan.

**OLIVA.** Leg broken in three places.

**BLANCA.** Oliva...

**MARIELA.** She thought if she were hurt enough, we would have to take her back to the hospital in Mexico City.

**OLIVA.** But we didn't.

**BLANCA.** Instead I lay in bed for six months here, with a large white cast on my leg.

**MARIELA.** And you never danced again.

**ADAM.** Wait, Blanca. Did you throw yourself into that well?

*(Beat.)*

**MARIELA.** Doesn't everybody?

**BLANCA**.  Papi wants flan and – he wants to meet Adam.

**MARIELA**.  You told him about Prof. Lovitz?

**BLANCA**.  Yes. And now my Papi wants to meet him.

**MARIELA**.  You told your Papi you were married, right?

**BLANCA**.  Yes.

**ADAM**.  Excuse me?

**BLANCA**.  I had to. It might upset Papi to know otherwise.

**OLIVA**.  It would kill him.

**ADAM**.  I see.

**MARIELA**.  The master lives and you get to finally meet him.

**ADAM**.  Now?

**BLANCA**.  I don't think you have much of a choice.

**MARIELA**.  Not a real democracy here like in the United States.

**ADAM**.  I haven't showered and –

**OLIVA**.  We have no water in the house tonight anyway.

**BLANCA**.  Let me get Papi a plate for his flan.

**OLIVA**.  I need to have a long talk with you, Blanca.

**BLANCA**.  It's the middle of the night, Oli.

**OLIVA**.  Virtue stays up 'til dawn.

(**BLANCA** *and* **OLIVA** *exit.*)

**MARIELA**.  Are you all right, Professor?

**ADAM**.  *(He's looking at the painting. Lost in thought.)* This painting has just been here since –

**MARIELA**.  Since the day my son died. Please Professor Lovitz, my husband awaits you.

**ADAM**.  I wish I could clean up.

**MARIELA.**  Stink is sensuous, Professor. At least that's what José says these days.

**ADAM.**  Well, I guess I'm sensuous. *(Beat.)*

**MARIELA.**  Let me show you the way.

**ADAM.**  Please.

**MARIELA.**  You realize you're about to meet the most celebrated member of the Salvatierra family?

**ADAM.**  Yes, I know.

**MARIELA.**  Are you nervous?

**ADAM.**  Yes, I am.

**MARIELA.**  You should be.

**ADAM.**  Pardon?

**MARIELA.**  It's dangerous to meet a dead man at night in the desert.

> (**MARIELA** *walks off and he follows.*)

# ACT II

*(Flashback. The ranch. **BLANCA** runs in. She is twelve years old.)*

**BLANCA.** Mami?

**MARIELA.** Carlos?

**BLANCA.** No. Just me.

**MARIELA.** Is Carlos still napping? Did you check?

**BLANCA.** Yes. He's sleeping.

**MARIELA.** Did you look?

**BLANCA.** Yes.

**MARIELA.** That little boy needs to rest. He gets so tired from his episodes. Did you lock the door again?

**BLANCA.** Yes.

**MARIELA.** We can't have our little boy running in this desert.

**BLANCA.** I did all the equations, Mami.

**MARIELA.** Good girl. Only three of them are wrong.

**BLANCA.** I wish I could go to school.

**MARIELA.** You are learning more here than you did in class.

**BLANCA.** Why are we are so far away from everybody?

**MARIELA.** I don't know anymore.

**BLANCA.** Oh. You know what I'm going to be when I grow up? When I grow up, I will always stand on the tip of my toes and dance as if I were water.

**MARIELA.** That's not an easy life. Being a dancer. Dancing is hard on your feet. Hard on your heart.

**BLANCA.** OK. I want to play house. Want to play?

**MARIELA.** I was up all night with Carlos. I am really tired.

**BLANCA.** Where's Papi?

**MARIELA.** In the barn. Painting,

**BLANCA.** He's just sitting. Staring at the canvas. I need him to draw me a house.

**MARIELA.** Well, don't bother him. I will draw one for you.

**BLANCA.** Will you?

**MARIELA.** Yes.

**BLANCA.** But you don't ever paint anymore.

**MARIELA.** Yes I do. I paint. Every day. All the time.

**BLANCA.** I never see you.

**MARIELA.** It's all in here. *(Points to her head.)* All my paintings.

**BLANCA.** Why don't you paint like other painters? On paper? *(Beat.)*

**MARIELA.** Because I don't mess with perfection. *(She laughs. BLANCA laughs a little too.)*

**BLANCA.** Is that funny?

**MARIELA.** No. I'm just tired.

**BLANCA.** Are you painting me? Right now?

**MARIELA.** Of course. Such a pretty girl. *(She lovingly touches BLANCA's hair. She stares at BLANCA.)* Why are you wearing those?

**BLANCA.** What?

**MARIELA.** How long have you been wearing those?

**BLANCA**.  I don't know.

**MARIELA**.  Those are my earrings.

**BLANCA**.  You never wear them. I thought you knew.

**MARIELA**.  How would I know?

**BLANCA**.  Because they are on my ears.

**MARIELA**.  Give me some paper. And those oil crayons.

> (**BLANCA** *does.* **MARIELA** *fingers the colors for a moment.*)

Now tell me what you want.

**BLANCA**.  My house, I want it to be magnificent.

**MARIELA**.  I expect nothing less.

**BLANCA**.  The house is in Mexico City. Not here. In the dirty desert. And I have the biggest room. In the middle of the house. And it's red. A red room. Yes! Oh Mami, that's so beautiful! And Carlos has a big room, but it's much smaller...smaller...that's right than mine. And its blue.

> (**MARIELA** *is electrified; it is infectious.*)

Yes. Oh that's so good! And Oliva has a smaller room and its green. Oh, Mami, that is so...so...wonderful. You're dancing with your hands!

> (**MARIELA** *is frantically drawing.* **BLANCA** *tries to grab the pencil.*)

Oh, I want to be a painter. I want to be a painter like you.

**MARIELA**.  You do?

**BLANCA**.  Yes!

**MARIELA**.  Are you sure?

**BLANCA**.  Yes!

**MARIELA.** I thought you wanted the house to be magnificent!

**BLANCA.** I do!

**MARIELA.** Then show me

(**MARIELA** *hands her the crayons and the pad.*)

**BLANCA.** We have a black dog...and a white cat...and rainbow birds. And I have a handsome husband with sky eyes. He's smart...but he thinks I'm smarter. And he looks at me all the time.

**MARIELA.** And where will you find this handsome husband?

**BLANCA.** I don't know. Where did you meet, Papi?

**MARIELA.** At the art school. He taught a class.

**BLANCA.** Was he a good teacher?

**MARIELA.** I took the class twice to see if he was.

**BLANCA.** Maybe I'll meet mine at school.

**MARIELA.** Maybe.

**BLANCA.** I want to show our drawing to Papi.

**MARIELA.** No.

**BLANCA.** Why?

**MARIELA.** It's not...not...finished. Besides, what about Papi and me? Our room.

**BLANCA.** Oh, you don't live in this drawing.

**MARIELA.** Not in this big fancy house?

**BLANCA.** You live in the desert.

**MARIELA.** That's a long way. The desert and here.

**BLANCA.** Oh, but you like it like that. You come over every time Carlos gets purple and crazy. But you take him outside. No screaming in my red house. He can only get crazy outside.

**MARIELA.** Carlos isn't crazy.

**BLANCA.** He runs and hits his head against the wall and cries and screams.

**MARIELA.** Everyone cries and screams.

**BLANCA.** Not you. Not ever.

**MARIELA.** Listen, instead of having Carlos in your fancy red house, why don't you let him stay with us here?

**BLANCA.** Because if Carlos lived with you, then you'd never want to visit me. *(Beat.)* So what do you think?

> *(Pause.* **MARIELA** *looks at the drawing. She sees something there that is promising, beautiful and upsetting to her.)*

**MARIELA.** Blanca?

> *(***MARIELA*** *gently strokes* **BLANCA**'s *face.)*

You can keep the earrings.

**BLANCA.** Really? Oh Mami! For me? I love them. Thank you.

**MARIELA.** You can keep my earrings…if you crumple the drawing. If you promise to stay away from the paint.

**BLANCA.** *(Beat.)* Is the drawing that bad?

**MARIELA.** Blanca, the drawing is beautiful. *(Beat.)* But you look very pretty with those earrings. And they are very valuable.

**BLANCA.** Why don't you want me to paint?

**MARIELA.** When I was twelve years old, my parents owned a large factory outside Monterrey. We lived in a grand house; my father bred fine horses while my fancy mother tried to breed me into a fine lady. But one day…I took my mother's favorite brooch. It had a red ruby in the middle and twelve Colombian emeralds all around. It was very expensive but I thought the red and green looked quite awful together…so I spent the entire afternoon prying the emeralds out.

**BLANCA.** Oh-oh.

**MARIELA.** That night, my mother discovered the brooch was missing and she and my father threatened horrible things to whoever was the thief. So I hid her broken brooch and said nothing. Two days later, my sweet nanny suddenly stopped coming. My parents had turned her into the police for stealing the brooch. After that, things happened. My nanny's family plotted revenge and the factory had a terrible fire. Unable to pay his debts, my father grew ill as the bank came and claimed the horses, the house, the furniture, the jewels, my toys...everything!

**BLANCA.** All over a stupid stolen brooch.

**MARIELA.** The ruby paid for my art school. And I sold the emeralds to buy my wedding dress. And I never had to be a fine lady again. *(Beat.)* Choose what you inherit very carefully.

**BLANCA.** I don't understand.

**MARIELA.** Do you want to be a painter?

**BLANCA.** Yes.

**MARIELA.** Do you want to have earrings?

**BLANCA.** Yes!

**MARIELA.** Do you want a rainbow colored house?

**BLANCA.** Yes!

**MARIELA.** A blue-eyed husband?

**BLANCA.** Yes.

**MARIELA.** And children?

**BLANCA.** I want them all. I want everything.

**MARIELA.** But sometimes you can't have everything.

Sometimes you just have to choose what is most important.

**BLANCA**.  And how will I know what is most important?

**MARIELA**.  That's something you will discover.

**BLANCA**.  *(Pause.)* I know what you chose.

> (**MARIELA** *tenderly touches* **BLANCA**'s *hair or touches her nose.)*

**MARIELA**.  What did I choose?

**BLANCA**.  *(Beat.)* You chose Carlos.

> (**BLANCA** *pulls off the earrings, gives them to her Mother and runs out with her drawing to show her Father.)*

Papi!

> *(End of flashback.)*

> *(José's room.)*

**JOSÉ**.  So she really brought a man to our house?

**MARIELA**.  She really did.

**ADAM**.  An honor to meet you. Señor. I'm Adam. Adam Lovitz.

> (**JOSÉ** *opens up his arms.)*

**JOSÉ**.  Adam! Adam! How wonderful. In the beginning – and there you are. Hug me, my boy. Mijo! Blanca tells me you teach a class in Art History at the University, right?

**ADAM**.  Right!

> (**JOSÉ** *envelopes* **ADAM** *in an affectionate hug.)*

> (**BLANCA** *and* **OLIVA** *come in with the flan.)*

**JOSÉ**.  And here comes my girl. My beautiful little girl.

**BLANCA**.  Papi, you met Adam.

**JOSÉ**.  Hugged him like a son.

**MARIELA**.  Blanca says they just got married.

**BLANCA**.  Yes! In a Church!

**JOSÉ**.  In white?

**BLANCA**.  Yes.

**JOSÉ**.  With cake?

**BLANCA**.  Yes.

**JOSÉ**.  But no family?

*(**BLANCA** looks at **MARIELA**.)*

**MARIELA**.  José, you were too sick to travel. Your little girl was just trying to make it easier on you.

**BLANCA**.  Yes.

**JOSÉ**.  Married!? To an American!? An American Art History Professor?!

**MARIELA**.  Who wants to write a chapter about you in his book.

**JOSÉ**.  *(Beat.)* You've done well, Blanca. *(He laughs.)*

**BLANCA**.  Papi – I brought water and flan.

**OLIVA**.  And a spoon.

**MARIELA**.  Blanca, you really shouldn't give him that.

**OLIVA**.  *(Holds up her hand.)* The effects are dangerous.

**BLANCA**.  Then why do you make it?

**JOSÉ**.  Please, give me some.

**MARIELA & OLIVA**.  José...

**JOSÉ**.  My daughter is home.

**BLANCA**.  Here, Papi. *(Hands him the plate.)* Do you want some, Adam?

**OLIVA.** There's only one spoon.

**JOSÉ.** He can share mine. Here. Eat flan.

(**BLANCA** *indicates to* **ADAM** *that he should.*)

**ADAM.** Well, if you insist.

**OLIVA.** Maybe sharing isn't a good idea...

**JOSÉ.** What can a gringo germ do to a man like me?

**OLIVA.** Let me just go get another spoon.

**MARIELA.** It's the Americans who get sick in Mexico, not the other way around, Oli.

**OLIVA.** You never know.

(**OLIVA** *exits.*)

**BLANCA.** I'm sorry. Oliva has her superstitious ways.

**ADAM.** That's all right.

**JOSÉ.** HA! Tempt fate, my boy. Here have some flan. Good, eh?

(**JOSÉ** *spoon feeds* **ADAM.**)

**ADAM.** Very good.

**JOSÉ.** Not only is she beautiful, my wife is a good cook.

See this is what a family should be! Mariela, come sit, close by. Adam!

**ADAM.** Señor!

(**MARIELA** *silently takes a chair and sits.*)

**JOSÉ.** My boy, you are a little older than I thought.

**MARIELA.** There's less of an age difference between them than between us.

**JOSÉ.** But you, my darling, were never a child.

**MARIELA.** And you, José, are never an adult.

**JOSÉ.** Semantics. So, you met Blanca at the University?

**ADAM.** Yes.

**JOSÉ.** Blanca and Adam. You make a dying man so happy.

**BLANCA.** Papi, you're not dying.

**JOSÉ.** Not tonight, anyway. Blanca come here. Sit here. Did Mami tell you? My blood's too sweet. I lost some of my toes already.

**BLANCA.** Oh, Papi.

**JOSÉ.** Gone. But I still feel them.

**ADAM.** Phantom pains.

**JOSÉ.** Yes! That's what they're called. Phantom pains. Another of God's sick little jokes. I like him. A smart American. Adam!

**ADAM.** Señor!

**JOSÉ.** A professor. Art History. You know, we had a lot of art history in this ranch at one point.

**ADAM.** Yes, Señora Kahlo mentioned it to me some months ago.

**JOSÉ.** You know Diego and Frida?

**ADAM.** I am helping Frida, writing the text guide for her exhibit in Paris. She's the first living woman to have a painting in the Louvre.

**BLANCA.** You know, Papi, I lived with them for awhile.

**JOSÉ.** Wonderful. Did you hear, Mariela? Our innocent daughter lived with that toad Diego. And our son-in-law knows our friends.

**MARIELA.** I'm hearing.

JOSÉ. When my wife was around twelve years old, she lived in Mexico City and took a short trolley ride by herself to go visit her aunt. That day, the trolley was very hot and full, and Mariela looked with envy at an older girl with dark braids sitting comfortably by the window, while she suffered, pressed against several smelly construction workers holding buckets of paint. Then a truck slammed into the trolley. WHAM! Bodies flew in the air, blood and gold paint splashed everywhere. Mariela did not suffer a scratch, but the girl, the girl with the braids was impaled by the pole in the trolley. Impaled.

Mariela watched in horror as they carried the limp bloody girl, laid her on a table and yanked that iron pole out of her. And to everyone's surprise, that girl screamed, lived, and became a famous artist. The lucky girl was Frida Kahlo.

*(Pause.)*

Success is all about chance, isn't it? Being in the right place at the right time.

MARIELA. That's why we are here in the desert, right?

JOSÉ. The Louvre! Little Frida is a great artist.

MARIELA. I thought she frightened you.

JOSÉ. Her art frightens me. I mean, seriously, I should be showing my work in Paris. Critics are idiots really. You excepted, professor, of course.

ADAM. Thank you.

JOSÉ. Yes, so Diego and Frida told you about when they came to visit us?

ADAM. A little.

JOSÉ. Not that long ago.

MARIELA. Nine years ago.

**JOSÉ**. Name a Mexican artist with a name and he was here. They all came here and we had a party here like the ones we used to have in Mexico City. They all came here to paint and be with us.

**MARIELA**. To eat our food and drink the last of our wine.

**JOSÉ**. It was wonderful! The desert is God's canvas, a place where all is possible. Do you remember Blanca, the painting, the dancing the music?

**BLANCA**. I was upstairs, stuck in bed, with the cast on my leg.

**JOSÉ**. Every room full of painters! All of this energy and excitement, Diego making jokes, Rufino on guitar! Everybody in the studio, in our old Barn, making challenges and eating and drinking and living! And what did Mariela do the whole weekend? What did she do? She sat in a corner, holding little Carlos in her lap, whispering in little Carlos's ear and saying nothing... nothing to any of our guests! Not one word. Nobody ever returned.

**MARIELA**. Carlos was frightened by all the people.

**JOSÉ**. You just didn't want to talk to anyone.

> *(Pause.)*

> (**OLIVA** *walks in, perhaps she has been eavesdropping.*)

**OLIVA**. I have another spoon! Oh.

> *(The flan is long gone.)*

**ADAM**. Thank you.

**MARIELA**. José, did Blanca tell you she's painting? About her exhibit?

**JOSÉ**. You are painting?

**BLANCA**. Yes, Papi, I'm painting.

**ADAM**. She has created quite a stir.

**MARIELA**. She had a series of paintings in a gallery. The paintings have each fetched three thousand pesos.

**OLIVA**. Blanca!

**JOSÉ**. Three thousand pesos? Each?

**BLANCA**. Yes, Papi.

**OLIVA**. That's a fortune!

**JOSÉ**. See Mariela? Our children did not need to be in school, getting germs from children and second-hand ideas from her teachers. Blanca is an artist. A living working artist! Three thousand pesos!

**MARIELA**. Tell me, Blanca, what kind of painting sells for that much?

**BLANCA**. *(Beat.)* Nudes of Diego Rivera.

**OLIVA**. God, please, no.

**JOSÉ**. If that son-of-a bitch exposed himself to my Blanca, I'll –

**ADAM**. Frida was there the whole time.

**BLANCA**. I painted him. Fat and old, naked and gray. Frida dressed in red, watching him, blindfolded.

(**OLIVA** *crosses herself.)*

**JOSÉ**. How ugly!

**ADAM**. Blanca is very talented. Watching her process was fascinating. She uses the brush like a fine knife, slicing color. Frida, standing firm and small, then Diego, naked and vulnerable, stripped and worried and wonderfully human. Señora Salvatierra, are you all right?

**MARIELA**. I would love to see those paintings with my own eyes.

**ADAM**. Your daughter is very talented.

**BLANCA**. That's what he says.

**ADAM**. But she's stopped.

**MARIELA**. You stopped painting?

**BLANCA**. It's just a dry spell.

**JOSÉ**. Just a dry spell? These spells, are cancer to an artist.

**BLANCA**. I just need the right inspiration.

**JOSÉ**. And here it is. The desert will awaken your senses again, fill your sight with images. For a true artist, the desert is an oasis.

**BLANCA**. I dream of this place all the time.

**JOSÉ**. Then, you should stay here.

**MARIELA**. What?

(**MARIELA** *and* **OLIVA** *share a look.*)

**JOSÉ**. Both of you. We have room. Professor you could think of this as academic research. You could interview me on the era, my approach, my friends, my paintings.

**ADAM**. Really?

**JOSÉ**. Yes. And you Blanca, could set up your easel and breathe and think and find your way out of this horrible "dry spell."

**ADAM**. That is a very gracious offer. An exciting proposition.

**JOSÉ**. Hell, I'm alive right? Might as well squeeze as much juice out of me while you can.

**ADAM**. Thank you, sir.

**JOSÉ**. Call me Papi.

**MARIELA**. José, they have lives in the City.

**JOSÉ**. I'm not holding them prisoner. It's just an invitation. We have room, right?

**OLIVA.** Yes...

**MARIELA.** Of course we have room,

**JOSÉ.** It would do me a world of good to spend my last days with my sweet daughter, giving her the inspiration she needs to go on.

**MARIELA.** Blanca and Adam are busy people.

**JOSÉ.** Don't you love your daughter?

**MARIELA.** Of course.

**JOSÉ.** So she can stay.

**BLANCA.** I have to say, Papi. The idea is appealing.

**JOSÉ.** This house is your home.

**MARIELA.** It's late.

**BLANCA.** We should go to bed. Goodnight Papi... Mami... Oliva.

**JOSÉ.** Good night.

**MARIELA.** Goodnight.

**ADAM.** A pleasure to meet you...alive, Señor Salvatierra.

**OLIVA.** Let me make sure you are each comfortable...in your own rooms.

**BLANCA.** Oliva, we aren't children.

**OLIVA.** Exactly.

(**OLIVA, BLANCA** and **ADAM** exit.)

**JOSÉ.** She came. She really did come.

**MARIELA.** I told you.

**JOSÉ.** Our baby girl.

**MARIELA.** What do you think of Adam?

**JOSÉ.** I hate him. Bad for Blanca. Bad for us.

**MARIELA**.  I thought you would be impressed. He knows about art.

**JOSÉ**.  I know about art. He knows nothing. Stupid Americans. They grab Texas, California, now Blanca.

**MARIELA**.  He likes Blanca's work.

**JOSÉ**.  Nudes of Diego Rivera! What kind of child paints something like that?

**MARIELA**.  Our child.

**JOSÉ**.  Even our daughter is wrapped up in ugliness. She needs to get away from that. To see the clean line of the horizon. To draw the curve of the sun's rays hit the sand. She needs to come home so I can teach her to be a real artist and to see the real beauty of the world.

**MARIELA**.  And what, witness the beauty of her father rotting in his bed? Dying limb by limb? Throwing tantrums and stabbing your sister with old forks? Is this how you want her to remember you?

**JOSÉ**.  Perhaps she will be able to see the beauty of my pain.

**MARIELA**.  The Beauty of your pain? Isn't that already slashed and hanging on our wall?

**JOSÉ**.  Mariela, shut the hell up.

**MARIELA**.  I'm sorry.

**JOSÉ**.  You are supposed to help the people you love.

**MARIELA**.  I do.

**JOSÉ**.  There's so many ways to destroy a man, and you've succeeded in so many ways.

　　　*(Pause.)*

**MARIELA**.  Adam, he's intelligent. He's handsome. He seems to love Blanca.

**JOSÉ**.  He wants my money.

**MARIELA.**  Your money is gone.

**JOSÉ**.  He wants my contacts.

**MARIELA.**  You have none.

**JOSÉ**.  He wants my daughter!

**MARIELA.**  Yes. And he wants to write a chapter about your masterpiece: *The Blue Barn.*

**JOSÉ**.  Get out! Get out!

>    (*Pause.*)

**MARIELA.**  I'll be in the other side of the door if you need something.

**JOSÉ**.  Wait. Stay. I'm sorry, Mariela. Stay with me.

**MARIELA.**  Good night.

**JOSÉ**.  Let me hear you breathe. I'm sorry. Please. –

>    (**JOSÉ** *follows her and falls down.*)

**MARIELA.**  José, are you all right?

**JOSÉ**.  Go to hell, you witch.

**MARIELA.**  I can help you.

**JOSÉ**.  I've never wanted you to help me.

>    (*Pause. He struggles.*)

I'm too heavy. Why do you feed me so much?

>    (**MARIELA** *stoops to help him.*)

**MARIELA.**  I can't –

>    (**MARIELA** *stumbles down with him.*)

I can't carry you.

**JOSÉ**.  I don't need to be carried. I'm a man. I just need a little push.

**MARIELA.** I'm trying.

**JOSÉ.** I know. *(Pause.)* I love you so much.

**MARIELA.** Thank you.

**JOSÉ.** And I know you love me too. Even when you hate me.

**MARIELA.** Especially when I hate you.

**JOSÉ.** You know, sometimes I think I see him, our poor baby boy.

**MARIELA.** You do?

**JOSÉ.** In my dreams, in the desert, I see him, running. Don't you?

**MARIELA.** You are sick, José.

**JOSÉ.** But I'm not crazy.

**MARIELA.** One of us is.

**JOSÉ.** Lift me up.

**MARIELA.** I don't know if...

                    *(Enter* **ADAM.***)*

**ADAM.** Is everything all right?

| **JOSÉ.** | **MARIELA.** |
| Yes. | No. |

**MARIELA.** José fell –

**JOSÉ.** I'm fine. What is this gringo doing awake?

**ADAM.** Let me help.

**JOSÉ.** I don't need your –

**MARIELA.** Grab him.

**ADAM.** Sr. Salvatierra –

**JOSÉ.** Let go!

*(They all stumble to the floor.)*

**MARIELA**.  That's enough, José.

**JOSÉ**.  I'm sorry. I'm sorry. I'll be good. I promise.

*(They drag him to the bed or wheelchair.)*

**MARIELA**.  Then let us help you.

**JOSÉ**.  Thank you.

**MARIELA**.  It's so late. You should go to bed.

**ADAM**.  I'm glad I could help.

**JOSÉ**.  You can't wait to get your hands on him can you, Mariela? Going to fuck the professor as soon as I fall asleep, eh?

**MARIELA**.  Good night, José.

*(**ADAM** and **MARIELA** leave José's room.)*

Thank you, Professor. I appreciate...

**ADAM**.  It was nothing.

**MARIELA**.  He's worse now.

Here, this will help *(She serves them both a drink.)*

Don't worry. I have no plans to sleep with you.

**ADAM**.  Señora Salvatierra –

**MARIELA**.  My husband likes to make others uncomfortable. And then he wonders why nobody comes and visits. Goodnight.

**ADAM**.  Señora...Mariela *(She stops.)* I wanted to apologize for my manner earlier.

**MARIELA**.  Please – don't.

**ADAM**.  I was hostile and rude in your own house.

**MARIELA.** It's the best conversation I've had in years, professor.

**ADAM.** I doubt that. *(Pause.)* It's so quiet here in the desert.

**MARIELA.** Except for the noises in your head. *(She laughs. Stops.)* I thought that was funny.

**ADAM.** I should check on Blanca.

**MARIELA.** Adam, why has Blanca stopped painting?

**ADAM.** I don't know. After she sold those paintings, she hasn't touched a brush or a canvas.

**MARIELA.** *(Beat.)* It's not so easy sometimes.

**ADAM.** Maybe staying here in the desert...would open her up.

**MARIELA.** Maybe.

**ADAM.** The scenery is quite captivating.

**MARIELA.** Very true.

**ADAM.** Without this desert there would have been no *Blue Barn* painting. No Presidential Grand Prize. Perhaps Blanca will find that inspiration she needs, here.

**MARIELA.** And you will be able to interview José, and write your chapter, in your new book.

**ADAM.** *(Beat.)* I heard you painted, once upon a time.

**MARIELA.** I beg your pardon?

**ADAM.** When you were younger. Before this ranch and the desert. You used to paint.

**MARIELA.** Is that what Blanca has told you?

**ADAM.** No. She never talks about you. It was Diego who told me that. He mentioned a painting. *The Bent Woman?*

**MARIELA.** *The Bent Woman.* Oh, yes.

**ADAM.** He told me its fierceness and frailty still haunts him.

**MARIELA.** Diego said that?

**ADAM.** Diego told me he wanted to trade one of his works for that painting.

*(Beat.)* But I guess, you weren't interested.

**MARIELA.** *(Pause.)* No. I guess I wasn't.

**ADAM.** Where is that painting?

**MARIELA.** It was destroyed in the fire...along with everything else.

**ADAM.** Why doesn't your husband want *The Blue Barn* in the National Museum of Fine Arts?

**MARIELA.** Because he wants it here. He came home from winning the Presidential Prize and put it up for all of us to see.

**ADAM.** He returned all of his prize money to buy it back from the museum.

**MARIELA.** It is a valuable piece.

**ADAM.** Then why didn't he sign it?

**MARIELA.** It wasn't really finished. Paintings are like children. They need to grow.

**ADAM.** *(Pause.)* You know what Diego says about the *The Blue Barn*?

**MARIELA.** "The Crown jewel of Salvatierra's work. A turbulent breakthrough in tone, style, and vision – José Salvatierra finds a new depth of feeling in his work, beautifully discovering the tender and brutal desolation of the desert."

**ADAM.** Actually, Tamayo said that. Diego says *The Blue Barn* is the best fucking thing José's ever stolen.

**MARIELA.** Stolen?

**ADAM.** Rumor has it that it's by some young man that came here to study.

**MARIELA.** José will love knowing you accuse him of theft.

**ADAM.** Oh, I don't. Just his peers.

**MARIELA.** Diego can't stand that he had to share the spotlight even if it was one minute with José.

**ADAM.** Why did José stop painting?

**MARIELA.** Carlos died...and Blanca went away. *(Pause.)* My husband is honorable. I promise you: José stole nothing.

    *(Enter **BLANCA**.)*

**BLANCA.** I thought you'd be sleeping.

**ADAM.** Your father fell.

**BLANCA.** No!

**MARIELA.** He's fine. Adam helped me get him back up.

**BLANCA.** Professor Lovitz can be very helpful.

    *(**BLANCA** leans into him, and kisses **ADAM**'s cheek – He is playful and loving toward her.)*

**ADAM.** You look tired, my dear.

**BLANCA.** Argh! Too many images racing through my mind. If I could only turn it off.

**ADAM.** You need to rest.

**MARIELA.** Blanca is a very talented girl.

**BLANCA.** You say that like it's a bad thing.

**MARIELA.** Not bad, just hard.

**BLANCA.** Yes. *(Pause...A moment of connection.)*

Sometimes I think I would rather have a good night's sleep.

**ADAM**.  Bite your tongue.

**BLANCA**.  These images are like smoke. The moment I try to grasp them they blow away.

**MARIELA**.  Maybe that's a blessing. Not every image deserves a canvas.

**BLANCA**.  So what then, I give up? And resign myself to living a plain and decent life and dedicate myself to raising children?

**MARIELA**.  Like me?

**ADAM**.  Ladies. It's late. We're tired.

**BLANCA**.  I want to see Papi.

**MARIELA**.  He's sleeping.

**BLANCA**.  I want to just make sure he's all right.

**ADAM**.  Maybe you should just let him have one good night's rest.

**BLANCA**.  Adam, don't tell me what to do. This is my house.

>    (**BLANCA** *tears off for José's room.*)

**MARIELA**.  I will speak with her.

**ADAM**.  Tell her, I'm awake, but have gone to lie down.

**MARIELA**.  Goodnight.

>    (*Flashback.*)

>    (**MARIELA** *and* **JOSÉ** *in the barn/studio.*)

**JOSÉ**.  Are you bringing me breakfast?

**MARIELA**.  Not yet.

**JOSÉ**.  Then go away!

**MARIELA**.  I'm just curious to see what you are working –

>    (*Beat. Dread.*) Oh, José…

(**MARIELA** *looks at the blank canvas.* **JOSÉ** *is despondent. Pause.*)

**JOSÉ**. I'm thinking!

**MARIELA**. Painting isn't about thinking.

**JOSÉ**. Don't quote me back to myself. It's just a dry spell.

**MARIELA**. How many paintings did the gallery commission?

**JOSÉ**. Twelve. Twelve paintings from twelve painters. They will pay me for a dozen paintings, like I'm some baker of bread.

**MARIELA**. And how many have you painted?

**JOSÉ**. Eleven.

**MARIELA**. José, you're almost done!

**JOSÉ**. I am done! DONE! DONE! DONE! Let them all go to hell. I'm not touching another canvas for them.

(**MARIELA** *touches him.*)

**MARIELA**. You are a talented man. You can do one more.

**JOSÉ**. I've painted eleven dreadful paintings that have to hang in a gallery with twelve paintings from Diego and Siqueiros and who knows who else.! Who do they think they are... I hate them.

(*Pause.*)

**MARIELA**. José, I think we need to move back to the city. We need to leave this desert.

**JOSÉ**. No!

**MARIELA**. This desert inspiration...this movement...is not going anywhere. José, we need to go back home.

**JOSÉ**. The Desert is our home.

**MARIELA**. You know Carlos is getting more difficult.

**JOSÉ.** We are not moving back to the city. Especially not now.

**MARIELA.** You are suffering. We are all suffering!

**JOSÉ.** We are artists!

**MARIELA.** We are a family.

**JOSÉ.** If we go back now, I will be the laughingstock of the entire community.

**MARIELA.** Nobody will laugh at you.

**JOSÉ.** Worse, they'll pity me. Or ignore me. But I am right. The Desert is God's Canvas! I have faith. I have faith in the art that will come from this desert.

**MARIELA.** If we go back, we can put Carlos in a special school. They can teach him things we can't.

**JOSÉ.** Learning happens here! Look at Blanca, she's reading university-level books and doing complicated math.

**MARIELA.** She was stuck in bed for six months with that awful cast! What else was there for her to do?

**JOSÉ.** We cannot move back.

**MARIELA.** Blanca threw herself into a water well. Carlos is banging his head against the walls. He wanders off. He will hurt himself.

**JOSÉ.** And he could hurt himself in the city at that fancy school you keep harping about. No! You, Blanca, Oli, and I can handle him.

**MARIELA.** Then why don't WE handle him? It always ends with one person.

**JOSÉ.** Children are not a problem.

**MARIELA.** In the desert they are! *(Beat.)* Carlos is beautiful and fragile.

**JOSÉ.** Fine, then send him away! Let him go.

**MARIELA.** *(Pause.)* Carlos needs to be with his parents.

**JOSÉ**. Yes, but Carlos' parents paint in the desert.

**MARIELA**. I don't paint anymore. And you – José – you are just sitting.

**JOSÉ**. It's a dry spell!

**MARIELA**. *(Hold up a brush.)* So paint one more painting! That's why we live in this God forsaken parched land... so you can paint. So paint! José!

> (**JOSÉ** *roars. He violently knocks down some easels and canvas. He makes a mess, then calms down.*)

**JOSÉ**. Nobody tells me what to do. Especially you.

**MARIELA**. The commission is incomplete. They won't pay you for eleven paintings.

**JOSÉ**. I know. I don't care.

**MARIELA**. A dozen paintings from a dozen artists. And you stop at eleven. They'll just pick someone else to show.

**JOSÉ**. So much the better. I don't care. I am the artist.

> (**JOSÉ** *starts to leave.*)

**MARIELA**. José, where are you going?

**JOSÉ**. To bang my head against the wall with my son.

> (**JOSÉ** *exits.*)

> (**MARIELA** *screams and covers her mouth. She is furious and frustrated. She begins to pick up after José's mess. Suddenly, she touches the blank canvas. She places it back on the easel. She rubs her bare palms over the rough surface. She steps back...and plunges her brush into some paint.*)

**MARIELA**. Molten blue.

(**MARIELA** *boldly brushes the paint onto the canvas. She makes another stroke and another...*)

(*The studio floods in blue light as she paints.*)

(*Lights out.*)

(*End of flashback.*)

(**BLANCA** *is watching* **JOSÉ** *sleep. She is singing him a song.* * **MARIELA** *comes in the room and starts braiding* **BLANCA***'s hair.*)

**MARIELA.** The professor is an interesting gentleman.

**BLANCA.** Yes, I love him very much.

**MARIELA.** But you are scared he will leave you.

**BLANCA.** *(Pause.)* I've stopped painting.

**MARIELA.** But he loves you.

**BLANCA.** Sometimes, I think what intrigues him about me is my paintings.

**MARIELA.** He is intrigued by you. Your paintings are part of you.

**BLANCA.** Are they? Really? My soul is a nude of Diego Rivera?

**MARIELA.** Several nudes, apparently.

**BLANCA.** Mami, you should have painted that nude of Diego.

**MARIELA.** What did you say?

---

* A license to produce *Mariela in the Desert* does not include a performance license for any third-party or copyrighted music. Licensees should create an original composition or use music in the public domain. For further information, please see the Music and Third-Party Materials Use Note on page iii.

**BLANCA.** It was your idea. Diego told me. That you tried to make a deal. That Diego would pose for you...if you posed for him.

**MARIELA.** How do you know that?

**BLANCA.** Frida has the nude of you up on her wall. It's beautiful.

**MARIELA.** I thought Diego would have sold it.

**BLANCA.** You posed for Diego but Diego didn't pose for you.

**MARIELA.** That was just a joke between your Papi and Diego.

**BLANCA.** It's not a very funny joke.

**MARIELA.** It is now that you painted Diego as naked as the day he was born.

**BLANCA.** You should have painted him.

**MARIELA.** You painted it. The painting is yours.

**BLANCA.** I painted it, but it doesn't feel like me. My whole new life, does not feel like mine. There's this girl, in Mexico City, that laughs, and loves, and paints and I watch her and realize I have no idea who she is. Where she came from. I'm so lost, I can't MOVE, I can't breathe. I can't paint! I sit at the blank canvas and stare.

(*Beat.*) How did Papi do it?

**MARIELA.** Do what?

**BLANCA.** Every time I put a brush on canvas... I think of *The Blue Barn*...of that green boy. Of that orange bird. And nothing-nothing – I've ever done comes close to being so beautiful and so true. How did Papi paint *The Blue Barn*? How did he find that inside of him? After so many years?

**MARIELA.** I don't know.

**BLANCA.**  How did he see I was an orange bird? How did he see that Carlos was green?

**MARIELA.**  He must have opened his eyes and looked.

**BLANCA.**  How did he know to smear the paint with such force to create such texture that the paint feels like the thick plaster of a cast?

**MARIELA.**  I don't know.

**BLANCA.**  How did he know to paint a red flame in the midst of it all?

**MARIELA.**  Blanca –

**BLANCA.**  How did Papi break away from a lifetime of seeing the world from the outside and see the world from the inside?

> *(Pause.)*

**MARIELA.**  Carlos painted the red flame.

**BLANCA.**  Carlos painted the flame?

**MARIELA.**  Yes.

**BLANCA.**  Papi let Carlos touch his painting?

**MARIELA.**  José would never let a child like Carlos touch his art.

> *(Pause.)*

**BLANCA.**  Oh God. *(Beat.)* Papi didn't paint *The Blue Barn*, did he?

> *(Pause.)*

**MARIELA.**  That painting destroyed our family.

**BLANCA.**  That painting is our family.

*(Beat.)* You're painting me right now, aren't you?

**MARIELA.**  Stay out of my head, little girl.

**BLANCA.** Look at me! Please look at me!

**MARIELA.** I don't need to look at you. I see you. I have you fixed in here.

**BLANCA.** *When I was twelve years old,* I lived in the bottom of a well in the desert with a little brother that cried all day, a father who cried all night, and a mother who never cried at all. Tonight I return to a home where my brother has long burned away, my father is sick and dying, and my mother...my mother...

(**MARIELA** *looks at* **BLANCA**.)

**MARIELA.** Yes?

**BLANCA.** ...is buried alive.

(*The wind blows.*)

**MARIELA.** Carlos –

**BLANCA.** It was a terrible accident.

**MARIELA.** He's gone.

**BLANCA.** When I look at that painting, Carlos isn't gone. I look at *The Blue Barn*, and I know exactly where my brother is. And I know who I am too.

(*Pause.*) Mami, did you paint *The Blue Barn*?

(**MARIELA** *looks over at* **JOSÉ**.)

(**BLANCA** *touches* **MARIELA***'s head. She kisses her Mother.*)

You do not always tell the truth, but I know you can paint it.

(**BLANCA** *exits.*)

(**JOSÉ** *inhales deeply and opens his eyes. He has heard everything. He is furious and accusing.*)

**MARIELA.** I thought you were asleep.

**JOSÉ.** *But I wasn't.* My chest is killing me.

**MARIELA.** You need your insulin. With all that's happened, I forgot.

**JOSÉ.** That hurts so bad.

**MARIELA.** I'll help you.

**JOSÉ.** I never wanted your help.

**MARIELA.** José –

**JOSÉ.** I sat down every day and cried and tried and tried until I painted this desert. You – you – stopped.

**MARIELA.** How else could we survive here like this?

*(Vicious, brutal, truth-telling.)*

**JOSÉ.** *I never told you* how they applauded. Diego! Frida! Siqueiros! All of them! How they got on their feet and applauded for me? And then they unveiled the Presidential Prize. *(Pause.)* So blue. So raw. And I stood up there, stared, and could say nothing. NOTHING! So the president shook my hand and babbled about inspiration and perspiration and thanked me for my fucking talent. *(Pause.)* A dozen artists each with a dozen paintings. All hanging in a great grand gallery. I only had eleven. You sent twelve. And out of the hundreds of paintings on the wall, the Academy chose one: one painting to humiliate me.

**MARIELA.** We should never speak of this!

**JOSÉ.** You painted *The Blue Barn* and then you sent it! Why did you send them your painting?

**MARIELA.** You needed that painting to complete the commission. You needed to show your work!

**JOSÉ.** *I* didn't need anything. *The Blue Barn* is about you!

**MARIELA.** We should have left this desert!

**JOSÉ.** We will never leave this desert!

**MARIELA.** Do not bring Blanca back here.

**JOSÉ.** This desert is God's canvas.

**MARIELA.** BUT we are not God!

**JOSÉ.** I am a man! A man with the ability to paint but with no vision. And then I have the folly to live my life with a woman who has a gift; a talent that festers in her head –

**MARIELA.** José, shut up –

**JOSÉ.** Do you know what I would have done if I had your talent?!! I would have led an artistic revolution. I would have changed the course of Mexican art!! There would be books, not chapters written about me!!! God gives you a gift and what do you do, Mariela? You waste yourself on a sickly boy, a decaying house, and keep that talent safe inside your head.

**MARIELA.** There is nothing safe inside my head! I want to dig my fingers into your chest and rip out your heart and paint these walls crimson with your blood! But your blood is too pale, too weak, too sickly to stain anything. You drag us all out here...for what? You talked about a movement, about a revolution, about making new art in the desert and we came and then you did nothing! You never killed a scorpion or pulled water from the well! You never danced with your daughter or held your son as he screamed!

You sat staring at empty canvasses in a dusty old barn while the rest of us drowned in this desert!

A real artist would have admitted the truth to himself, held his head high, and led us out of this dry, dry land! God forgive me, I should have tried to get us out sooner.

**JOSÉ.** The desert did not fail us! *The Blue Barn* is a masterpiece!! Your masterpiece!

**MARIELA.** Carlos is dead!

**JOSÉ.** And why did he die, Mariela? Why? *(Beat.)*

Don't you see, my love? Your painting did not kill Carlos. No!

*(Beat.)* Your mothering killed our son.

> (**MARIELA** *drops the insulin and then crushes it under her foot. Amazed silence.*)

Dear God.

> *(Silence. She looks at him.)*

**MARIELA.** My God.

**JOSÉ.** I didn't know I could still get to you, Mariela.

> (**MARIELA** *turns and starts to leave.*)

Where are you going?

**MARIELA.** *(Back in* **MARIELA** *mode.)* I need to get another bottle of insulin.

**JOSÉ.** Mariela, no.

**MARIELA.** *(Beat.)* José...you need...

**JOSÉ.** I cannot paint. My son is gone. The only masterpiece of my career, is yours. And now my fiercely talented daughter, a gifted artist like her mother, knows her father is a fraud. I am dead.

**MARIELA.** Oh, Jose.

**JOSÉ.** Nothing is more beautiful than a decisive woman, Mariela. *(Pause.)*

And you look very beautiful right now. The curve of your chin. The fold of your dress. The curl of your hair. The perfect portrait.

> (**MARIELA** *hugs* **JOSÉ** *passionately.*)

**JOSÉ.** I loved Carlos.

**MARIELA.** I know.

**JOSÉ.** I love Blanca.

**MARIELA.** I know.

**JOSÉ.** I love you.

>    (**MARIELA** *kisses* **JOSÉ** *tenderly on the lips.*)

**MARIELA.** Good-bye, José.

**JOSÉ.** Goodnight, Mariela.

>    (**MARIELA** *gets up and closes the door behind her. She goes outside.*)

>    (*Flashback. The Old Barn.* **CARLOS** *enters.*)

**CARLOS.** Mami?

**MARIELA.** Baby, it's the middle of the night!

**CARLOS.** What are you doing?

**MARIELA.** I'm sending some of your father's paintings to a very important gallery.

**CARLOS.** (*Looks at the canvas.*) Oh, look, Papi painted our barn. It's Blue.

**MARIELA.** Do you like it?

**CARLOS.** That boy, that's me.

**MARIELA.** Yes.

**CARLOS.** Because he's green. And that orange bird is Blanca.

**MARIELA.** Yes.

**CARLOS.** Papi doesn't paint like this.

**MARIELA.** No, he doesn't.

**CARLOS.** He paints the outsides. This is the insides.

**MARIELA.** Do you like it?

**CARLOS.** You should send this painting.

**MARIELA.** Oh, it's not finished. See? It's unsigned and it's missing something.

> (**CARLOS** *grabs a paint brush and paints a red line.*)

Carlos!

**CARLOS.** It needed red.

**MARIELA.** Carlos!

**CARLOS.** It's a red flame.

> (**MARIELA** *stares at the painting.*)

**MARIELA.** Wait. Fire is just what the painting needed.

> (**CARLOS** *begins to fall apart.*)

**CARLOS.** Papi is going to be angry. Papi is going to be angry.

**MARIELA.** Baby, it's all right.

**CARLOS.** I hurt his painting.

> (**CARLOS** *takes the brush and fervently sweeps it up and down his face. Bewildered lines of blue or red. He starts pacing.*)

**MARIELA.** Carlos, you didn't hurt Papi's painting.

**CARLOS.** He says we shouldn't touch and I touched it. I painted. *(Moans.)* When he sees it he will…*(Moans.)*

**MARIELA.** Papi won't see it. Look, I'll send it with all of these.

> (*Slides it in with the other paintings.* **CARLOS** *calms.*)

It's gone. That painting is going far away to Mexico City. Papi will never see what we did.

(**CARLOS** *suddenly goes to the door.*)

**CARLOS.**  I want to run in the desert.

(**MARIELA** *stops him.*)

**MARIELA.**  No. You cannot run in the desert. We might never find you.

**CARLOS.**  I want to run!

**MARIELA.**  Me too. But I don't run, I hide. You should hide too! Hide here in the barn.

**CARLOS.**  But what if the scorpions hear me?!!

**MARIELA.**  Then this trunk! Yes, hide in there. Look how nice it is. It's quiet and dark and safe. The scorpions will never hear you in here. Climb in.

**CARLOS.**  It's nice and dark. (*He closes himself in.*)

**MARIELA.**  Carlos, when you are afraid, do not run in the desert, come to the barn and hide in this trunk. Then Mami will know where you are. Then Mami will come and get you.

(*End of flashback.*)

(**OLIVA** *and* **BLANCA** *tell* **ADAM** *the story.*)

**OLIVA.**  It was the year José finally had an exhibit in a great gallery in Mexico City. *The Desert Series.* That's what the press called it. We started getting news. His name said in the same sentences as Rufino Tamayo and Diego Rivera. Then we heard one of José's paintings won the Presidential Prize and would hang in the National Museum of Fine Arts. José was ecstatic. Singing, bouncing off the walls with pride. We all were. And he went to the city and we waited...

Something must have gone terribly wrong in Mexico City because when he came back...On the day he came back – José stood in the doorway like a bull, sweating and smelling of kerosene. He silently walked in as if we weren't there and put up the Presidential Prize: a blue barn, with a little green boy, an orange bird, Then, through the window. So quickly, so fast. I saw the studio was burning. We turned to do something –

**BLANCA.** But Papi's voice stopped us, "Let the barn burn." So we all watched, mesmerized by this crazy fire that was tearing down that odd Barn...while Papi just looked at the Presidential Prize and whispered "Now that piece, that's inspired. That's art" and for a moment everything was. The fire: crackling blueness and red flames and black smoke. It was windy and wicked and beautiful. Until Mami softly said:

**BLANCA & OLIVA.** Oh God, where is Carlos?

**OLIVA.** The barn, the paintings, the boy, all gone. Grey ashes, bent metal, and small charred bones. José walking around screaming like a hollowed man. Mariela sitting as still and quiet and cold as the desert.

**BLANCA.** That is when I went away.

**OLIVA.** Heaven knows why that cursed picture won. Carlos is not a green boy. You are not an orange bird.

**BLANCA.** *(Beat.)* But, we are.

**OLIVA.** Only God understands artists.

> *(**MARIELA** enters, she looks distraught.)*

**BLANCA.** Mami, is everything all right?

**ADAM.** Señora Salvatierra, your lip is bleeding.

> *(**MARIELA** suddenly goes up the* The Blue Barn. *She takes it and gives it to **BLANCA**.)*

**MARIELA.** Blanca, I want you to take this. It's for you.

**BLANCA.** *(Pause.)* Thank you, Mami.

> *(**MARIELA** touches **BLANCA***'s face.)*

**MARIELA.**  Promise me you will paint again.

(**BLANCA** *is speechless.*)

(*Beat.*) It's been a very long night. You and Adam should get some sleep. Goodnight.

**ADAM**.  Yes. Goodnight.

**BLANCA.**  Goodnight, Mami.

**MARIELA.**  Goodnight, Blanca. Goodnight Adam. I'll see you both in the morning.

(**BLANCA** *holds the painting. She and* **ADAM** *exit.*)

**OLIVA.**  I'm so tired, too.

**MARIELA.**  You should get some rest as well, Oliva.

**OLIVA.**  I'll just check on José before I go to sleep.

**MARIELA.**  Oliva – José is dead.

**OLIVA.**  What?

**MARIELA.**  José is dead.

**OLIVA.**  Oh no! No. My poor brother (*Beat.* **OLIVA** *pulls herself together.*) We should tell Blanca, and Adam.

**MARIELA.**  Not now.

**OLIVA.**  Mariela –

**MARIELA.**  We will tell Blanca after she wakes up.

**OLIVA.**  (*Beat.*) I'd like to sit with him and pray.

**MARIELA.**  Of course.

**OLIVA.**  Goodnight, Mariela.

(**MARIELA** *hugs* **OLIVA**.)

**MARIELA.**  Thank you, Oliva.

*(**OLIVA** kisses **MARIELA**'s forehead and exits.)*

*(**MARIELA** is alone. It is dark.)*

*(She places her hands in her face and weeps.)*

*(**CARLOS** walks in, perhaps in a pool of green light. He is happy. He is whole.)*

Carlos?

**CARLOS**. Yes, Mami.

*(Pause. **MARIELA** drinks in the presence of her son.)*

**MARIELA**. Oh Carlos... I've missed you.

**CARLOS**. I've been running in the desert! Everything is full. I am not afraid.

**MARIELA**. Carlos, you are so beautiful.

*(A look between Mother and son.)*

**CARLOS**. The sun is coming up.

*(Dawn begins.)*

*(**CARLOS** reaches for his pocket and pulls out a paintbrush.)*

*(He holds out the brush to his mother.)*

*(**MARIELA** looks at his outstretched hand for a long time. **MARIELA** takes the brush.)*

**MARIELA**. Well, my love, today I am going to paint.

**CARLOS**. Can I stay with you?

**MARIELA**. Of course. I cannot begin without you.

*(**MARIELA** sweeps her brush.)*

*(Blue paint, like water, streaks the entire stage.* **CARLOS** *whips a red color.)*

*(Perhaps we see a green boy, running, and an orange bird, flying away.)*

## The End

www.ingramcontent.com/pod-product-compliance
Lightning Source LLC
Chambersburg PA
CBHW070351120726
47909CB00008B/2801